Crystal Wilkinson

Blackberries, Blackberries

The Toby Press, *London*

First published in 2000 by
The Toby Press *Ltd, London*
www.tobypress.com

ISBN 1 902881 34 6 (PB)

A CIP catalogue record for this title is available from the British Library

Designed by Fresh Produce, London

Typeset in Garamond by
Rowland Phototypesetting Ltd., Bury St Edmunds

Printed and bound in Great Britain by
St Edmundsbury Press Ltd, Bury St Edmunds

For Silas and Christine

Contents

Acknowledgments

To my three brown sugar babies—Gerald, Delainia and Elainia; Mama Dorisy Jean Anderson; Cousin/Sister Darlene Warner; my sista friends—Daundra Scisney-Givens, Pat Tatum, Deborah Chambers, Donna Johnson, Joan Brannon, Nikky Finney, Opal Baker, Kelly Norman Ellis, Lula Mae Fragd and Cookie Hall; the Affrilachian Poets, who cuddled my words and helped me make them sing; Frank X. Walker, my 729, my brother, who took me by the hand and brought me out of the writing closet; LaVon Van Williams Jr; George Anthony Ellis Jr; Wendel Price; the Carnegie Center for Literacy and Learning, where I find home and family always; the Kentucky Foundation for Women; the Kentucky Arts Council; Marie Brown; Lesley-Ann Brown; Marita Golden and the Zora Neale Hurston/Richard Wright Foundation; Aunt Lo; Debra and Trish; and all those unseen but felt, those who gather with me around my journal books and my computer making the words come; I am forever grateful to y'all for tugging, pushing and lifting me when I was about to fall from center.

An Introduction to Blackberries, Blackberries

I grew up on a farm in Indian Creek, Kentucky, during
the seventies. I swam in creeks and roamed the knobs and
hills. We had an outhouse and no inside running water.
Our house was heated by coal and wood-burning stoves
and we lived so far back in the woods that we could get
only one television station. But it was a place of beauty—
trees, green grass and blue sky as far as you could see. I am
country.

Being country is as much a part of me as my full lips,
wide hips, dreadlocks and high cheekbones. There are many
black country folks who have lived and are living in small
towns, up hollers and across knobs. They are all over the
South—scattered like milk-thistle seeds in the wind. The
stories in this book are centered in these places.

As a girl, there was an extreme urgency to grow up as soon as possible. Being a woman was something that I longed for. I remember sitting quietly watching the way my grandmother put on lipstick, circling her lips just so. I studied my mother's walk, how it changed when she was all dressed up for church. I eavesdropped in on "women's business". Listened to the music my aunts and older cousins made with their voices. Observed the way my cousin's hand rested in the deep curve separating her waist and hip while her other hand moved in the air when she was most passionate about something. I watched how these beautiful women wore their countryness, wore their womanness. How they interacted with men, children and each other. I wanted to learn all the ways of womenfolk, to capture all the secrets. What I didn't know then was that a woman's life is never cut and dried. Never plain and simple, not as a girl, not as a full-fledged woman.

These stories come from the ordinary and the extra-ordinary. From black, country women with curious lives. From struggle, from fear, from love, from life, from the gut, from the heart. Black and juicy, just like a blackberry.

Music for Meriah

The summer after she left her mama's house, Meriah Clay began watching Osmond play piano. Sometimes she attended his small jazz performances alone. When she went with her girlfriends, they would let Osmond's fingers massage a week's work, listless children or manless beds out of their lives. He would stretch himself along the length of the piano, his legs spread wide, his big brown hands reaching across the horizon of the instrument. Most of the time all they could ever see was the back of his balding head and the sway and twist, sometimes hunch, of his shoulders. Occasionally if they sat at a front table and strained their necks, they could see his face contort, his eyes close, his head throw back. He always dressed plainly. Khaki pants. A white collarless dress shirt. No tie. He wasn't a lovely man in any extraordinary sense. Average size, average height. Just average. The friends were never captivated by the mere sight of Osmond. But when they heard him play, the women sitting round the table would begin to nod and roll their eyes until each woman, even without words, knew what the other was thinking. And the boldest among them would say, "G-i-r-l!" And draw the one-syllable word out like a preacher's shout and every woman at the table would giggle or cut their eyes toward the bold one as if to say *Amen*.

Meriah always *said* it was the music she came for. She had loved jazz since hearing her daddy's records when she was a little bitty girl. But that was long before her mama had driven her daddy first to drink, then back to New York with her nervous ways.

During breaks, Osmond would come to Meriah's table and thank her for coming. She would introduce him to her friends, and watch as he mesmerized them with the lilt of his accent and his closed-mouth smile. Meriah would lean back in her chair, confidently sipping a glass of wine, her right pointer finger and its companion pressed underneath the curve of the wineglass, her pinkie hoisted in the air.

Meriah herself was only middling. Plain. Twenty-eight years old. A recent escapee of her mama's possessive clutches. Not too much makeup. Just heavy burgundy or cinnamon lips and the occasional brush of mauve eye shadow above the lids. Her hair was in dreadlocks. She wore it neat, twisted up in a bun or pulled back with a headband. She preferred long, loose, natural garments that covered her ample body. Meriah never wore jewelry to work, but always wore rings on her fingers and large bangles around her wrist when she frequented the nightclubs and bars where Osmond played. She fancied herself looking more experienced, more worldly, when she dressed this way. She imagined herself reminding Osmond of home. But she wasn't even exactly sure where *home* was. She thought Osmond's accent was Caribbean but never gathered the courage to ask. She just knew he wasn't from Kentucky, which added to the intrigue.

It was Thursday and none of Meriah's girlfriends was up for going out on a weeknight. She sat alone at the Jockey Café and waited for Osmond's Trio. She fidgeted with the mushroom crêpe appetizer she had ordered to accompany her wine. She felt out of place. The room was full of Lexington's élite. The occasional Kentucky horse-owner celebrity. The college football coach and his wife. A table of young chattering white women, in designer clothes and expensive jewelry, flipping hair and throwing eyes at any available bachelors in the room. An elderly couple sat in the corner. Meriah watched them eat their dinner. The man was dark-skinned. Tall and thin. Frail-looking. Black suit and tie. His hair a dapper sprinkling of salt and pepper. The woman—short and stocky. Chartreuse suit. Pinned near her neck was a cameo brooch that bobbed up and down when she spoke or ate. Her head was covered in soft, red hair with tufts of gray around the roots. Fluffy. Reminded Meriah of strawberry cotton candy. Meriah was close enough to see the matching wedding rings on the couple's fingers. She wondered what their lives were like. She couldn't keep her eyes away from them for long.

5

The man reached across the table and placed his bony dark hand upon the woman's fleshy, paler one. Just as the woman cast her portly glance toward Meriah, the flesh beneath her chin wagging, a large white spot of light hit the small stage. Osmond and the rest of the trio walked onto the platform. Meriah's stomach fluttered in anticipation. A singer joined them, wearing a shiny silver dress. Underneath the spotlight Meriah could see the woman's makeup was piled on in layers, two shades lighter than it should have been for her coffee-bean skin, and a curly, auburn wig sat slightly askew on her head. But her voice was good. A deep, scratchy good. Meriah watched Osmond place his fingers on the keys, sometimes lightly, sometimes firmly. He always reminded her of the best of her former lovers. Every gentle touch, every soft kiss she had ever felt was offered back to her through some movement or expression that Osmond made. She crossed her legs and watched the bend and sway of him caress the piano.

During the first break, the jazz woman plopped herself down into a chair at Meriah's table. "Enjoyin the show, baby girl?" she rasped out. Her breath was heavy with liquor. Meriah nodded, *yes*, bobbing her head so hard that she could feel her earrings hit the sides of her neck. "I been on the road, singin most all my life," the singer said, placing her shiny, silver shoes in another empty chair at Meriah's table. "These feet achin up a storm. Wasn't always like this." The singer lit a long, filtered cigarette and blew smoke above Meriah's head. "You from here, girl?" she asked.

"Yes ma'am," Meriah managed. "All my life."

"Lord, girl, you better get out and do you some livin."
The woman's voice rose to a cackle and she pushed her
hand toward Meriah in jest. Then she reached over and
patted her on the arm, like a mama would do. "Better get
on out of here and live, girl. Life don't come at you but
one good time. And I know there ain't too many good
times in Lexington, Kentucky." The woman's words were
the opposite of Meriah's mama's. Her mama always urged
her to stay close. Never to leave. "Ain't nothing in those
big cities you're always talking about that you can't find
right here," she said. "You've just got roaming in your
bones. You *are* your daddy's child made over."

"You got kids?" The singer tapped her cigarette on
the edge of the ashtray.

"No," Meriah said.

"Man?"

"No."

"Ain't got no excuse then." The jazz woman's voice
droned on about her children and the husbands that
fathered them.

* * *

At eighteen Meriah's bags were packed and her plane ticket
to New York was bought until her mama's hysteria had
convinced her to stay. "Your daddy left me and now you
too." Her crying, screaming mama, tears streaming down
her face, had clung to Meriah like a desperate child. "If
you are leaving, then you might as well shoot me," she had
said. "Kill me dead right this minute because it will be the

last of me." Meriah put her arms around her mama. Placed every dream and hope of her own upon a shelf. Her daddy was gone. But she had stayed behind to be swallowed up by her mama's misery. Swallowed up whole by her mama's propensity to smother.

* * *

Meriah was looking but trying not to look for Osmond. She caught a glimpse of the couple. The man looked at the woman and she looked back. Their fingers were interlaced across the table. The woman looked in Meriah's direction again, then looked away. Meriah caught Osmond in the corner of her eye talking to the table of young white women. He must have seen the jazz singer at her table and decided to talk to them. A wave of panic began to rise in her stomach.

8

"Anything in particular you want to hear, sugar?" The singer was now standing, hovering over Meriah, waiting for a response. "Let me do somethin just for you." As she bent, Meriah could see her breasts. Dark, wrinkled and sagging, about to fall from the silver dress. A withering body much like her mama's yet this woman had the slightest hint of something young wiggling deep in her gut.

"Request?" she asked over her shoulder. "Last chance."

"*God Bless the Child,*" Meriah said.

The woman propped herself on the stool and leaned over to whisper something in Osmond's ear as he resettled himself on the piano bench. She slipped the remainder of the cigarette into a glass of water.

"Here's your song, girl," she said into the microphone and pointed a crooked, arthritic finger toward Meriah. Osmond twisted his neck toward the audience and threw his closed-lip smile toward Meriah. The woman's voice and Osmond's touch on the keys took Meriah to a place that she could not come back from. A place she didn't want to come back from. She was comfortable in that place. Just nestling there.

*   *   *

Five years after Meriah's daddy had left, he came to visit her. They were not allowed to leave her mama's house. Meriah was fifteen and she and her daddy sat arm in arm on the back porch. She carried the smell of him with her even now. The smell of a freshly ironed shirt even through the sweater he wore. The slightly musty smell of a man. When he told her he would always love her, *no matter what,* she had cried into his arm. Her mama had stood at the door, her arms folded into herself, with fear in her eyes. When Meriah had hugged and kissed her daddy goodbye, she had seen her mama's mouth twist. In that instant, with the November wind at her back, a great loathing for her mama had blown in with her daddy's leaving.

*   *   *

During the second break the jazz singer winked at Meriah but spent her time entertaining the couple. Meriah could see them, first listening carefully, then laughing loudly at something the woman said.

9

Osmond joined Meriah. "Thank you for coming," he said. "Good to see you again."

"Always a pleasure," Meriah said, trying to still the flipping insides of her stomach. "Always a pleasure," she repeated and swirled her wine around in its glass.

"Did you enjoy your request?"

"Real nice," she said.

"We're at the Pearly Peacock Saturday night," Osmond said, his lips curling up at the corners, the Caribbean lilt cradling Meriah in its open palm.

"Oh, up on Lime?" she said, feigning ignorance.

"Corner of Lime and Mill," Osmond confirmed as he stood up. The smell of him, his spicy cologne, wafted up and around Meriah's head, landing in her nostrils and staying. Settling in. As he passed between the chairs behind Meriah, Osmond placed his fingertips firmly on her shoulders. And she could hear the swish of his pants against her chair. "See you Saturday night," he said giving her shoulders a slight squeeze before heading back to the stage.

*   *   *

When Meriah returned home her cat, Moon, weaved circles in and out of her legs as she made her way through the small apartment. She scooped Moon in her arms, then flipped on all the lights, including the bathroom light. Somehow with the lights all on she felt less lonely. She brushed the clutter to one side of the kitchen counter. A half-eaten bag of apple chips. A small junk mail pile had formed beside the telephone. Half a loaf of moldy bread. Beneath it all she found a lone can of cat food. She placed Moon on the counter and allowed the cat to climb among the disorder while she opened the can. The hungry cat purred in anticipation, knocking a few pieces of mail to the floor and shaking the bread bag open. Meriah left the mail on the floor and left the bread undisturbed. She filled the pet dish with two heaping spoonfuls of food. Sat the cat down and placed the leftovers in the refrigerator.

She checked her messages. One from her mama recited an entire list of *what you need to dos* including the regular *come back home*. Her mama's message ended with a pleading, "Call me, Meriah Lynn Clay. You call your mother, right now. You are worrying me to my death." The second message was from the office. It was her supervisor who said she had decided to take another vacation day and that Meriah would have to *hold down the fort*. "Always holding down the fort," Meriah scoffed. Meriah left Moon to fend for herself and began to undress on her way to the bedroom. Her shoes were deposited in the living room near the couch, stockings on the doorknob. Dress and jewelry piled on the chair.

11

In her bed Meriah tried to conjure back that feeling of Osmond's fingertips on her shoulders, the squeeze. She tried to call up the scent of his cologne. The *swishing* sound of his pants. The rhythm of the sway of his body and his hands across the piano's keys.

* * *

Saturday night as Meriah readied herself for the Pearly Pea-cock, the telephone rang. She instinctively reached for the receiver but decided, at the last moment, to let the machine pick it up. Her mama's voice came screeching into the box, "Meriah, Meriah, I know you there. Meriah, Meriah, pick up this phone right now this minute." Meriah was in the bathroom, at the sink, brushing her teeth. As her mama's words bounced off the apartment walls, she held her ground until the tone changed. "Baby," her mama said. "Please pick up the phone, Mama just wants to talk to you. Okay? I just want to know that you're okay."

"Hello, Mama."

"Good, oh thank goodness. Are you all right?"

"Fine, Mama."

"Are you eating okay?"

"Yes."

"Need anything? You know you . . ."

"Mama, I know I can come home anytime. I know."

There was a silence. A moment of discomfort between the women. A huge band of dissatisfaction that reached from the house on Hampton Street clear to the other side of town down the hallway and into the bedroom in Meriah's apartment. Meriah let out a long, laborious sigh.

"Will you come by for dinner tomorrow, Meriah? I'm fixing meatloaf and new potatoes."

"We'll see, Mama," Meriah said. "We'll see."

"Work okay?"

"Yes, Mama."

"That cat, Sun or . . ."

"Moon is fine, Mama. Well, I've got to go."

"I love you, Meriah. See you tomorrow?"

"I love you too, Mama. We'll see. Bye."

*   *   *

A hunger clicked into the Pearly Peacock on the heels of Meriah's shoes as she sauntered toward the table. She threw out her hellos around the table and scanned the room for first sight of Osmond. She ordered first a strawberry daiquiri, then a good red wine. The four women talked, and left their med-clerk chatter tucked away beneath plunging necklines and inside elastic girdles. The women all nodded toward Meriah when Osmond entered the room. Then they broke out into an embarrassingly unified howl of laughter like schoolgirls and all six eyes focused on Meriah. Meriah laughed, too, but coyly covered her mouth. When the music began, a quiet tapping of feet, the bobbing of heads and the occasional drumming of fingers on the table, replaced talk. Meriah focused her wonder on Osmond. His fingers gliding, the way the muscles in his back rode each note.

During one of the breaks, Osmond made his regular visit to Meriah's table and stood behind her while he spoke, the tips of his fingers again resting on her shoulders. "Ladies," he said, nodding his head toward the other three women. "Welcome to the Pearly Peacock. Are you enjoying yourselves?"

"Yes," two of them said in unison.

"Uh huh," the bold one said, lowering her voice to a throaty growl.

Osmond cleared his throat. "And you?" He bent his head forward into Meriah's face.

"Wonderful," Meriah said, her eyes darting nervously away from him.

By one o'clock two of the women, who had children waiting to be picked up, had left. Meriah and the remaining friend sat filling themselves up on wine and music. A familiar face haunted Meriah from the corner. Tall and lanky. A charming smile. Billy Martin. Meriah had met Billy at the shoe store where he worked. He had helped her pick out shoes. Meriah's mama had glared. "Not those," she had dictated. "She will fall." Billy had cupped the small-heeled pump in his hand, like it was the Cinderella slipper, then placed it on Meriah's foot. His hand had intentionally lingered on the ball of her foot before he slid it into the shoe. When her mama wasn't looking, Billy had dropped his phone number into Meriah's bag. She had slipped from her bedroom window to meet him. He had been Meriah's first lover. She had tried to learn how to sexually please a man. How to relax and be pleased. It was the everyday of a relationship, the part that sun shines on, that she hadn't yet come to understand. Billy had ended it when Meriah had refused to quit sneaking behind her mama's back. To do things that normal couples did. Meriah was content to keep slipping through the shadows, picking up what bits of freedom she could muster there. So he had left her, too. Now, there he was. Billy Martin. In the corner, his arm looped around the shoulders of a small, delicate woman the color of butterscotch pudding. After Billy there had been

Darius, an investment broker from the third floor of the office building where Meriah worked. He had been the one who had helped her gain the confidence to leave her mama's house. They had planned, during Meriah's lunch breaks, for her to lease an apartment on the south side, far from her mama, furnish it, and then Meriah was to simply leave for work and not return home. After she moved out, her mama had called the police. Attempted to file a missing persons report. She incessantly called Meriah's office, first demanding then begging her to come home. Meriah had moved out in the fall. By the new year Darius, too, had stopped calling. Stopped coming by. Meriah watched Billy and the butterscotch woman. Once, he even looked in Meriah's direction. The two held a gaze for only seconds. Then Meriah looked down and Billy looked away, slightly embarrassed. There wouldn't even be a casual handshake. No kind of acknowledgment that they knew one another.

At the end of the night Meriah was reeling. After her friend had left, after Billy and his woman had left, after the club had just about cleared, Meriah remained. She watched Osmond and the other musicians clear the stage. Osmond returned to her table, wiping sweat from his brow, a towel thrown across his shoulder and a bottle of water in his hand.

"You all right?" he said, bending down close to her and patting her shoulder. "A little too much to drink?"

"I'm fine," Meriah said, at first looking into his eyes, then glancing away. "Fine," she repeated.

"See you next time?" Osmond said turning and wiping his forehead with the towel.

"Next time," Meriah repeated after him.

Meriah sat in her car in the back parking lot of the Pearly Peacock. When Osmond started his car, she started hers. The hunger she had brought into the Pearly Peacock earlier in the evening had grown to starvation. In traffic, she stayed a few cars behind. She followed Osmond through downtown, across the county line. He made a left turn into a subdivision and so did she. She watched him pull into a driveway in front of a large white house. She drove past, so as not to be noticed. Down the street with the lights off, Meriah watched Osmond enter the house. Once the house began to light up, she could see through the open blinds that it was nicely furnished—art on the walls, art deco furniture. Meriah found her way to the porch, her finger reached out to ring the doorbell but she couldn't. She stopped to touch the scripted lettering of his name engraved into the shiny gold mailbox. She crept along the side of Osmond's house, happy to see that he had an abundance of flowerbeds. Meriah imagined herself gardening there in the spring. Osmond would call out to her, *Baby, I'm home,* and she would run into his arms. She found her way to the back patio and rested on a chair, trying to find some nerve. In the darkness she could see herself in a bright yellow dress, Osmond by her side, sipping iced lemonade, sweet tea maybe. Now she could see Osmond through an upstairs window. A shadowy figure, his arms up over his head removing his shirt. Meriah's heart beat a little faster. Then she saw that he was not alone. A woman joined him near the window, their arms wrapping around one another. The two silhouettes danced for a minute in Meriah's view, kissed, then disappeared.

*   *   *

Sunday night, when the moon was yawning its way up, Meriah stayed in bed. The answering machine, sitting on the edge of her dresser, flashed her mama's concerns. Eight messages. Meriah had put herself to bed and stayed there all day. She tried to wrestle her thoughts away from Osmond. Away from Billy Martin and his butterscotch woman. Lying there beneath the covers, wide awake, reminded her of when she was a little girl, before her daddy left. And the two of them, her mama and her daddy, would stand over her bed when she was sick. In their house there was always music. Always jazz. Monk, Miles Davis, Strayhorn, Coletrane. She could see her daddy's face, his handsome, bearded jawline, his sleepy brown eyes. Her daddy's job was to make her smile. He made clown faces, stretching his face out, sticking his fingers in his ears, sometimes tickling her. Her mama was the worried one, testing her forehead for fever. Pursed mouth and a frown etched between her eyebrows. But for the first time in a long time she remembered her mama's smile, too. Bright white teeth beaming at her. Flashing at her daddy between full cherry lips. Her mama had been the one who brought her lemon and honey for her sore throats. Always the one who climbed into her sickbed and held her close. The one who made her feel safe. Meriah rested her head on the pillow and tried to reel that memory in. She grabbed a hold of it and cradled it like something precious.

17

Later that night she picked up the phone and dialed her mama.

"Hello, Mama," she said.

"Meriah, I was worried to death. Worried sick that something had happened to you."

"I'm okay, Mama," she said. "I'm okay."

The next evening, Meriah's mama enveloped her like some over-protective hawk. Meriah stood stiff and unyielding at first, lingering at the door step. Then she embraced the husk of the woman who had raised her. Meriah could feel the hump in her mama's back. The thinning of her bones. And in one fleeting moment she envisaged her dead.

"I was so worried," her mama said. "You're all I have."

"I know," Meriah said. "I know."

After dinner Meriah sat quietly as her mama fingered each of her daddy's records. Together they sat, neither of them speaking, the jazz playing. Her mama's fingers moving over the posed faces on the covers. Meriah watched her mama grow tired and fall asleep on the couch, the albums strewn all around her like lily pads. For the longest time she listened in the dark. She listened to the in and out of her mama's breath as it danced through her daddy's music and did not even think of leaving.

The Awakening

Autumn Marie Hicks was fifty-four, not a young woman coming to this decision.

But life was calling something fierce to her that morning. Kissing on her ear, life was saying, "Come grab a piece of breath again."

Autumn Marie and Clancy had known each other all their lives. She had decided she would marry him when she was just seven years old. Clancy was six. They had lived side by side over on Mason's Ridge. Their mamas worked together cleaning up houses and their daddies worked together down at the flour mill.

Autumn Marie, a girl with pigtails flying, had said to her mama, "I'm gonna marry Clancy Hicks one day." She smiled now at the clearness of that memory. Her mama tasting the greens cooking in the pot. Her grin appearing from around a wooden tasting spoon. "Now child," her mama had said, "what makes you think that boy's gonna marry you?" And they both had laughed. Autumn Marie had loved the spirit in her mother, always like sunshine and dew drops. She laughed out loud, looked over and saw she had not disturbed Clancy at all. Laughed again at the notion of his ever waking up before her.

Each morning she would get up early, get the coffee on, get breakfast on and still have time to come back to bed. Clancy would be awake, pretending to be asleep. She'd climb in the bed with her back to his. Then he'd roll over and kiss her neck from behind, rub his fingers up and down her arms, across her breast and eventually make his way in between her thighs. She'd roll over to meet his kiss. They'd bring the morning in dancing, knowing what music each other wanted to hear. Autumn Marie would close her eyes and still see daybreak coming in the window.

She now stared at Clancy's back, trying to figure out how long that had been. She remembered the first time she'd rolled over and stared at his back, waiting, thinking he was pretending. It seemed a hundred lifetimes after that. She strained her memory for the wet of his kiss.

Clancy went out to work every day. On Friday nights he would go down to Ron's Shack and drink beer until Ron would have to call a taxi to take him home. When her mama was alive, Autumn Marie would spend every late Sunday afternoon sitting on a stool in her mama's kitchen, being a little girl again. But now her mama was dead. And she had grown quite tired of being everybody's something. She was Clancy's wife. The kids' mama, but her own nothing.

She eased out of Clancy's bed. Got dressed. Grabbed a blanket and slipped out the door. Morning in Clancy's house found her gone. She walked into town, went straight to the dress shop. Used the light-bill money to buy herself a new dress. If Clancy could have Friday night beer, she could have a Thursday dress.

"Autumn Marie you going somewhere special?" the dress-shop woman said, eyeing the bright yellow sundress that she had picked out. Autumn Marie and the kids had been there enough for the dress-shop woman to know that Clancy didn't allow nobody in his house to wear yellow or red. Called them the devil's colors.

"I sure in the hell am," Autumn Marie said, leaning on the counter. "And give me that lipstick, the red one, and that face powder too."

Autumn Marie slipped into the gas-station bathroom. Put on her new dress. Tried out the face powder and 'Rowdy Red' lipstick. She took wet toilet paper and wiped off the looking-glass so she could get a clear picture of herself. She was pleased.

I might be brown as a ber-ry but that's only secon-dary. And you can't tell the difference after dark. I may not be so appealing but I've got that certain feeling. And you can't tell the difference after dark . . . She started singing to herself real low. Made her feel like she was Alberta Hunter for real. She closed her eyes and pictured herself strutting in the beer joint and Clancy's eyes falling out of his head and his mouth hanging open for the flies to land in.

She walked through town slow. Menfolk said "howdy do", like she was new in the place and she just strutted on.

She walked through town and over to Mason's Ridge. It was the inside of summer and the sweet williams made the breeze smell so good that Autumn Marie could taste it in her mouth. She sat on what used to be the front porch of her home place and talked with her dead mama.

Mama, it's like I ain't got no spirit. Like it's all rotted out like leaves in the dirt. I'm just the washer woman. The cleaner woman, the mama, the wife, the cook. The kids think I'm the food and money machine. Clancy talks at me. But I don't think he can even see me. I'm a husk of what was.

Autumn Marie cried on the porch, aching for her mama and some glimpse of herself until she was all cried out. When the sweet williams breeze blew again and broke a chip off her pain, she breathed deep every bit. Raised herself up from the porch and headed to a path down by the creek. All the flowers—the honeysuckle, the lilies of the valley, the daisies—seen her coming and nodded their heads. She walked slow, fingering every petal, touching every living thing along the way, conscious even of the up and down of her step upon the earth.

At the creek's edge, she unfolded her blanket and crawled into its middle. She unbuckled her shoes and unzipped her new dress, letting it fall around her ankles. She stretched as far as she could in every direction. Then removed her panties and brassiere. She tipped her toe into the creek, followed by her all. The water was warm. Her load lightened. She removed the lipstick and powder from her face. Rubbed water all up and down her body.

She returned to the blanket naked, her eyes closed tight. She didn't see a vision of Clancy or the kids or her dead mama. She saw herself smiling and at peace, content. Slowly she rubbed her fingers across her face, inside her mouth, across her breasts and up and down her legs. Her velvet hands gave honor to herself and places unseen, untouched for what seemed like a hundred lifetimes. She closed her eyes and still saw evening coming across the sky.

Hushed

He is her secret keeper. At night they sneak from different directions. They meet at the creek that snakes across the bottom of the fields, a natural divide of the earth. They are kin, distant cousins. She thinks he is beautiful, especially when the moon dances light onto the curls of his hair and she imagines she sees his reflection smiling back. His skin is silk and, like hers, the lightest of browns, like fine oak. His eyes: shiny, the color of buckeyes.

Everyone thinks he is ignorant, that he is dumb, but he is not. Our brother and sister laugh at him. They think it's funny that he is mute. Funny that only whispered sounds come out when he speaks. In many ways, Naoma is mute, too. The quiet one, the deceitful one, Mama says. Sneaky, Mama says when she's mad at her. Spiteful, Mama says to

Naoma when she finds a large piece gouged from the hot milk cake. Naoma has always courted the shadows to avoid being slapped in the face or lashed with a belt. She has never done any more or any less than the rest of us, yet she has always been the one that Mama singles out. Tana, our sister, has stolen as many pieces of chess pie or lemon cake as Naoma has. We have all shirked our dish duty. Alphonso, our brother, has broken his share of vases and tea cups. And although Naoma is neither the eldest nor the youngest, Mama always shouts her name when the clothes fall from the line into the dirt. When the toilet overflows. When she finds the broken glass. When the kitchen has not been swept. When she needs her sassafras tea. Pap sees but doesn't see. He keeps his head turned. He walks away.

In town, over cups of coffee and across clotheslines, the rumor floats through the jaws of old women that Pap is not Naoma's real father. I have always been too afraid to ask, too afraid to know. But every time Mama hits her or twists her mouth to call Naoma's name, every time Pap looks the other way, I know she must be somebody else's child.

Naoma suffers in silence as I imagine Clifton suffers in his. Almost every time I shut my eyes, I see brother, sisters and cousins encircling Clifton and taunting him— running behind him, where they know he cannot see what they are saying. I can see in his eyes he is tortured. Naoma stands with her eyes toward the ground when the laughing begins. But in the night she assures Clifton that he is no laughing matter. They have come to know each other's ways. Between them silence is virtuous.

In our small house on Jones Knob Naoma thinks everyone is asleep. She leans over to test our baby sister. While she is snoring, she blows air into her face. It takes her breath away like a baby or puppy. She gasps for air and in her slumber tries to brush Naoma from her cheeks. She looks like an angel. Her face is round like the moon, the color of burnt bread. It is only at night, when she is asleep, that I truly love her. Naoma stands over her awhile. I like our sister this way. Sleep makes her more like Naoma. In the day she wears our mother's mouth and eyes. Naoma fights the urge to kiss her on the lips and tiptoes from the bedroom.

She prepares a picnic basket for Clifton. Inside a bucket, lined with a clean tea towel, she places two cold ham biscuits, some leftover potato cakes, a Granny Smith apple, a baby jar full of sorghum molasses, and a mason jar of sweet tea. In the darkness of the kitchen she moves quietly, like some nocturnal cat, moving only in shadows and moonlight.

She smoothes her dress and places a quilt roll under her arm. She has dressed in red. Clifton is partial to brilliant colors. He carries Naoma's purple scarf in the pocket of his jeans so that she is always with him. Mama says red is the preference of old whores and fast-tail girls. Naoma has scented her neckbone with Mama's dusting powder.

Clifton knows to meet her at midnight. All the cousins were helping out in the field today. Pap, sensing Naoma had some way with Clifton, asked her to take him to the barn to help put up the cows. Everyone laughed, including

Pap. Inside the barn, I saw Naoma kiss Clifton's lips. She told him to meet her at twelve. He watched her lips move but she pulled a tobacco stick from one of the stalls and wrote a big twelve in the dirt to make sure.

Naoma came home to supper with too big a smile on her face. Mama, as usual, has her own suspicions but she would never guess Clifton, in anybody's million years. Mama says she can see the *whore* coming out in Naoma, can see it in her eyes and the spread of her hips. "Hot in the ass," she says when Naoma walks by.

After supper, I watched Naoma looking at herself in the looking-glass. She walked back and forth in front of it, staring at herself from different angles. I tried hard to find some gleam of the whorishness Mama swears she sees. I found nothing whorish but nothing that says sixteen either.

Outside, the night air is barely cool. A shiver tingles through my bones, somewhere between fear and anticipation. In the bright moonlight, a huge shadow stretches alongside Naoma as I follow in the bushes. It is a bit frightening at first, but as I reach the curve in the dirt road, I am comforted by my blacker self spread out across the ground. Naoma slows her gait and looks up at the night sky. Above us is an endless sheet of blue-black velvet sprinkled with a million stars. I think we must be the only girls in Kentucky partaking of this wonder.

As we near the creek, I hear frogs croaking and katydids scatting. I hear Naoma's feet crunching the gravel. She arrives before Clifton and spreads the quilt across the rocks as close to the creek as she can get. The sound of water gurgling lulls me. Naoma reaches her hand out and lets the water run through her fingers and down her salty arm.

I hear Clifton long before I see him. I hear his feet crunching through the brush, then gravel giving way under his feet. When Naoma stands to greet him, he bears on her a full open-mouthed kiss. Above his lip is the beginning of a mustache. Clifton is twenty-one, yet I think of him as being much younger. His face is fresh and full of sweetness, like that of a small boy.

His left arm is wrapped behind his back, sheltering a surprise. When he brings forth his open palm, I see it is red and white candies wrapped in clear cellophane. As Naoma unloosens one from its package and pops it into her mouth, Clifton removes the tea towel from the bucket. He brings the ham biscuit up to his nose, smells, then bites. Of course, he doesn't speak but I see in his expression the pleasure that good food brings.

Clifton and Naoma lie on their backs, sandwiched between their own quilt and the one that blankets the sky. They eat, rising up on their sides to sip the tea. They embrace and Naoma kisses each of Clifton's deaf ears and the soft skin along the sleek line of his neck. He reaches his hand along her thigh under the skirt of her dress. He fingers the fabric. A tingle vibrates, chills my bones. I shiver and know that he must hear it somewhere from the inside out.

Clifton and Naoma lie face to face in the dark. We are all quiet like prayer. Our hushed voices pierce the night air.

Girl Talk

Now I'm not one to get too involved in much girl talk but being the only boy in the house, sometimes it just can't be helped.

We live up on Water Street, just above the slaughter house. In my house it's me—my real name is Bruce but my family calls me Brother and my boys call me Butch— Ma Mae, Mama and Hattie Lee. Now you won't catch me saying too much about Hattie Lee cause it would have been all right by me if she'd never been born.

But like I was saying Ma Mae and Mama are always talking about something. Usually they have Hattie Lee all tucked up under them cooking or quilting or fixing their hair. Usually, unless it's supper time, lunch time or time to go to bed or church, I steer clear of the whole bunch and hang out down on the lot with my boys. But every so often I get an earful, when I'm in Mama's kitchen helping peel potatoes or carrying in groceries.

This morning things didn't start out too good cause Mama called me back to the house four times when I was trying to get to school. The first time she wanted to check my face to see if I'd washed it good. Then just when my foot was about off the last step of the porch she was handing me my homework. Then when I got to the end of the sidewalk she was hollering that I should wait on Hattie Lee cause girls shouldn't have to walk by themselves, and the last time was to give me sugar.

If that wasn't enough, I walked Hattie Lee to her class at the second grade building—you see, I think all seven-year-old little girls should be kept locked up somewhere till they get old enough to know how to act—and she's hanging all over me, trying to hold my hand. And I'm thinking about pushing her down and realize that if I get her dress dirty then Mama's gonna be hollering all night about it. So I grab her hand before she falls. Just when I get her steady and I am about to jerk away from her again, here comes all my boys around the corner and Jude gets to hollering, "Look at Butch holding his little sister's hand. Ain't that cute." And they all— Jude, Stephon, David and Gary—start laughing.

"Aww, shut up Jude, that's why yo mama's so fat it took ten of y'all to bring her to the breakfast table this morning," I holler, running off from Hattie Lee.

"Don't even want to start," Jude says. "Yo granny's so black she thought the skillet was a mirror."

Then Gary says, "And yo mama's so ugly she thought a june bug was her daddy."

"Boy, you are gone," I say to Gary and slap him in the back of the head.

"Man, you corny," Stephon says.

"Corn-ny," Jude and David say at the same time, slapping each other five. They always do that.

"Bye, Brother," Hattie Lee says as I'm running away from her.

"Bye, go on in your room," I holler back, still running with my back turned cause I know she's standing there looking stupid.

We all bust through the sixth grade room at the same time and go our separate ways. We've all been best friends since kindergarten but in the classroom we've been split up since then, too. The teachers think it's best that way. Seems to me like a boy could learn better if he was sitting close to his boys but I guess they don't think that way.

English, science, math, and then at lunch I'm sitting at the isolation table, because I was spitting peas through a rolled-up piece of paper at some girls at lunch yesterday, and I miss out on talking up an after-school plan. You see me and my boys sit together at lunch and plan on what we gonna do after school. Sometimes we head for the lot to play kick ball, sometimes to our hangout down by the creek and sometimes to somebody's house.

So I'm sitting at the isolation table and here comes old gap-toothed Debra Jean Hoskins sitting by me. "Mrs Johnson told me to move over here cause I hit Jude, your friend Mr Horseface, with a paper wad." Like I care. I can tell she's mad and about to cry. Girls are the only ones that cry over isolation and getting called out and silly mess like that. "He hit me first and she didn't say nothing about that," she says, her voice getting that crackly sound like girls do right before they start acting a fool crying.

God, I'm thinking to myself, don't I get enough of this at home. Everytime you turn around there's a girl in the way. Can't even be in trouble by yourself. I pulled my tray down as far as the bench would go and spent most of my lunch with my hand under my chin.

The day didn't get no better. I had forgot that today was gym day and so when I dressed out in my shorts, my knees was all rusty cause I didn't put on lotion this morning. So I'd play a little while then run to the bathroom and rub water on my knees. It worked til I got to playing and the water dried and my knees were just as rusty as before. I guess it worked though cause nobody noticed. At least I don't think they did.

So the day finally ended, the school bell rang and we all walking home. Hattie Lee's about four steps behind us and we're kind of planning as we go. "Let's go down to the lot," I'm saying.

"No, let's go play video games over Stephon's," Gary says.

"Yeah, we can take turns playing Centipede," Stephon says.

"No," Jude and David say at the same time. They always do that.

So we went to the lot cause it was closest and we didn't have a plan no way. Right beside the gate stood John F. Kennedy Jackson. We all in our bluejeans and t-shirts and he's standing there all pressed and pretty like he's going to church, complete with a bow tie and little tam on his head. John F. don't get out much on account he's sort of a cripple. Walks funny with a limp. I always thought it was all cause he was named after a president that had been shot and killed. That somehow he got a hold of some of that cursed luck through the name. Ma Mae and Mama says its cause he was born too early. They say his mama had to rub coal oil and dirty dishwater on his legs for near a year before his legs got straight enough for him to be able to walk. Mama says he could do better "if his silly old mama would let him out the house to run and play like normal".

Like I said before, I don't participate in girl talk but in my house you ain't got much choice. So the boys surrounded John F. and just sort of stared at him awhile.

"Y'all gonna play ball today," he said.

"Yeah," we all said at the same time.

Then Gary opened up his big old stupid mouth and said, "You want to play with us to make it even?" We had never worried about making even teams. Sometimes we played two against three and sometimes three against two.

"Yeah," John F. said and I got nervous. Mama and Ma Mae says that you can't go messing around with only children had by old women. They say if it's the only child and the woman's old then that means it took her whole life to have a baby and that's probably all she ever wanted in the world. So she's gonna treat that baby like it was gold and keep it by her side always.

And that John F. sure was Miss Beulah's gold piece.

She always had him shined and polished decorating something. He decorated her car while she was in the grocery store. He decorated her house cause he didn't go to regular school, she taught him at home. He was always right beside her at church. She never would even let him in the children's Sunday School class. He was always with her with the grown folk. In the summer, he decorated her porch, dressed up all pretty like a statue on the porch, eating cookies and drinking lemonade, when me and my boys walked by heading toward the lot.

I was real curious why he was out off the porch today and I wasn't too excited about playing with him. Had nothing to do with his legs. Wasn't that we didn't let outsiders into our club. Every once in awhile we'd even let Hattie Lee run some bases when we was desperate but I just didn't know. Just had an odd-ball feeling.

We drew blades of grass to choose captains and played rock, paper, scissors to see who chose first. Me and Jude got captains and Jude got firsts. He picked David like usual and I picked Stephon. Then Jude picked Gary and I got John F.

Things didn't seem too bad. John F. played good outfield and even with his hobble he ran pretty good. He even passed to me to help get Jude out making that three and our turn to kick.

I kicked, then Stephon. We was both on base. It was

John F.'s turn to kick. All he had to do was kick it out far enough for us to run home and we'd have some points. So anyway, David rolls him the ball. John F. kicks the ball straight up and it comes back to him like a boomerang and hits him right in the nose. He laid straight out in the dirt like somebody gone to bed.

So here we are standing over him like he's a dead squirrel in the road and he opens his eyes and is kind of grinning up at us. His nose is pouring blood and we all just staring at him. Then Miss Beulah notices he's missing off the porch and looks down at the lot and sees us all standing over him and comes flying down the sidewalk.

"Oh, my Lord. Oh, my Lord. Lord have mercy they done killed my baby!"

She's running and hollering and John F. raises up a little and is still grinning all silly like he's proud of a bloody nose. His tie is all crooked and his nose is still gushing the blood.

Miss Beulah comes up and yanks us all away and drags John F. back to the porch and into the house, crying, tears running down her face, and screaming like he was dead all the way.

And I'm thinking John F. sure is her gold piece but I think he'd be more happy being somebody's copper penny.

Me and the boys all looked at each other and Hattie Lee's pulling on my sleeve cause she wants to go home.

"Brother, I'm bout to go on myself," she says.

I'm walking her home, waving bye to my boys, thinking they ought to visit their mamas' kitchens more often. Then they'd know about these things.

Chocolate Divine

Leon Slade was dark, silk like chocolate. Hair
glistening, shining like the sun even in the dead of night.
A confectionery smile that made all women melt like hot
fudge on ice cream. Lips smooth, natural lines drawn around
them, made just for kissing. That man made a flutter go
through women's hearts wherever he went. Charisma, Aunt
Tene used to call it. Me, I'd call it something else altogether.
Aunt Tene always said that everything good to you ain't
good for you. And I guess somebody musta made up that
saying just to go alongside Leon Slade.

It was a Saturday night, when all this started. I guess
a whole buncha things done got started on a Saturday
night. Seems like a good time for a lotta folks' troubles to
begin.

Leon eyed hisself in the mirror. Chocolate supreme. The face, that of an Egyptian king. "Go head, man," he said to hisself, throwing a pretend high-five in the air.

That Leon was something else and knowed it. Sweet as sugar in the morning good looks. He sprayed cologne around his neckbone, imagined some woman smelling the scent as she kissed his neck and headed on out the door. Now usually Leon would have headed on over to the Barn in Boneyville. That's right, the Barn and that is just what it was, a barn. Now I don't see how nobody says that folks from the country ain't smart. Country folks got plenty of sense cause somebody from down in Boneyville, which is bout as country as you can get, had got the bright idea to take their old barn, cement the floor and turn it into a nightclub, complete with a genuine bar, plenty of good music, food, flashing lights and all. Leon decided that night that the women at the Barn had seen too much of him so he headed over to the Ponderosa in Danville, which was an old restaurant, I think, or an old something or another. It didn't start out being what it was. But it was a night club now. Boy, black folks come up with some stuff now. But it worked and still works to this day. So, on this particular Saturday night, Leon decides he needs to give the women over in Danville a piece of the pie.

You ever heard that saying that everybody in the world got a twin someplace? And if ever Leon Slade had a twin it was June Gatton from over in Harrodsburg. The only difference was that one was a man and one was a woman. Just the difference to bring them together.

June eyed herself in the looking-glass. Mahogany perfection. The face, could pass for thirty. Black don't crack. She rubbed more foundation on just in case. She puckered her lips toward her looking-glass self and nodded, yes, to the fiery red lipstick, whore-red Aunt Tene would say. June always had young boys to grown men calling her "sexy chocolate". She was a dark-skinned sister, face smooth as glass. Unblemished. Wide eyes with long black eyelashes that shot a look that would give a man the shivers. Her forty-year-old hips gave shape to the second skin that was the slinking black dress she had caught on sale at the mall. Her hair, died jet black, cut short and young, looked good. "Go head, sexy chocolate," she said out loud to herself. She ground her hips into an invisible dance partner to a slow jam that came cross the radio. She walked away from the mirror looking over her left shoulder at her behind poured in that second skin. "Oooh weee, shake it sexy chocolate," she said. Slipped her stocking feet into black suede pumps, patted her own backside in approval and headed for the door. Headed straight on over to Danville to the Ponderosa.

When June stepped up on the party, she came in like nobody's business, laughing way too loud just in case everybody didn't see her. She was hollering, "Why hello there! Hey girl, ain't seen you in awhile," and all that sort of thing to people she didn't even know. Then she headed to the bar for a glass full of something she didn't have no business drinking. The room, that's really all it was, a room, was full of forty-something-year-old folks trying to be eighteen or nineteen again. Music loud, teenage loud; people who didn't remember the moves, dancing up a storm, at least trying to; and even a couple in the corner kissing each other up, making it a forty-something-act-like-a-teenager-and-make-a-fool-out-yourself-or-somebody-else type of affair for sure. Smoke curled up about the ceiling, backs were slapped and women straight from the hairdresser sported spandex and knit, stretched cross forty- and fifty-year-old bodies. Men, with hats on crooked, eyed something they already knew about like it was something new. But that was the Ponderosa on a Saturday night.

Leon was already there working the party. "Go head on man," he says almost at the top of his lungs to a normal-acting brother sitting on a piece of couch in the corner. More than likely the man didn't even crack a word Leon's way but gave him a high-five anyway to help the brother keep his game going.

Now June was the type of woman who had been around the bend a few times and knew trouble when she seen it coming and that night trouble, by the name of Leon Slade, walked right up on her from across the room almost first thing. They couldn't help but spot each other. Sorta like looking in a mirror. They both was acting up such a fool that they was dividing the room on attention. Part of the people was staring at Leon do his thing. The other half concentrated on June. So Leon thought he'd check her out.

June saw him gliding her way and steadied herself against him and was ready to give it right back as fast as it came cause she sure knew how. But Leon came on over to her, said, "I'm Leon" with that special look in his eyes, licking his sexy lips when he knew she was looking. He was talking his stuff, really just his regular stuff. "Damn, baby, you sure look good tonight," he says looking straight down the front of her dress.

"Name's June," she gives right back, "you looking kinda fine your damn self." And she looks him down, stopping you know where, and looks him up again. They go on with all this sorta thing back and forth. And June was being as cool as a cucumber. But before she knew it, she gets to thinking bout how smooth his skin is and sure nuff like a chocolate bar that she could take a bite of and how that natural line goes around them big lips of his. So she tries to think about how everything good to you ain't good for you, cause it was certainly more old women than Aunt Tene that had handed out that advice, but it all goes right on out the window. June turns away from Leon to talk to some other man looking her up the backside but Leon puts his arms around her and pulls her real close. She can smell the cologne on his neckbone. She tries to think of something smart to say. Something extra shocking, extra smooth but a slow jam starts playing and he gives her that grinding slow dance she was daydreaming about. His hands rest on the lower curve of her back right in the danger zone and he rubs up and down her back while they dancing, fingering that slinking black dress. Pow! Melted just like hot fudge on ice cream.

Now I can't say much bout women falling for men they know ain't no good for them, happens all the time. But June was supposed to be one of the experts.

43

That night, that Saturday night, June and Leon ended up at June's place wrapped up in a ball of supreme delight til the sun shined its last rays in her bedroom window late Sunday evening. June fell for Leon like mad and they, with they fine selves, became a couple. They was seen in the park holding hands and passing sugar at the Barn and the Ponderosa on Saturday nights. They got even more attention as a couple than they did alone. They was like a bolt of lightning coming in a room. Heads jerked up to take a look. They both enjoyed that. Leon's eyes would wander past June every so often. He even flirted with women when they was out together. He would wink at another woman past June's shoulder, fix his special stare on her til he had her full attention and just when the woman got to the melting stage and was getting her hopes up, he'd turn his attention on back to June.

June knew what kind of rollercoaster she was riding and was trying not to be no man's fool, so to get Leon back, she would walk back and forth past the bar and make too many trips to the bathroom just so the menfolks could see what they was missing. She still craved the "sexy chocolate" calls but just as soon as she got one while Leon was looking, she would go on back and snuggle up side him.

This went on about a year. And right when all them men and women was bout to give up on the both of them, Leon called it quits. He just woke up one Sunday morning at June's house and told her so long. Said he loved her but he just wasn't no settling man. June changed, I'm telling you. She moved on over from being the craved to being craver. She followed Leon from the Barn to the Ponderosa, just eyeing him like all the other women. She never caused a scene though. Just stood back, her heart aching every time she saw another woman headed out the door with Leon. June still got plenty of attention, though some tiny crows feet had begun to form at the edge of her eyes. But she couldn't pay them other men no mind. She didn't even hear them calling when she walked by. June craved Leon like a chocolate sundae, followed him around with loss in her heart. She craved that man's sweetness. Not the kind of sweetness that comes straight from a man's heart but that sticky, rich, sweetness he reeked of. Like the too-sweet chess pie cooked in Aunt Tene's kitchen. That nasty, too-sweet sweetness that tells you that one delicious piece is more than you can stand. And Leon went on about his business of turning every woman's eyes but every once in a while when June craved that chocolate that he could offer, he'd head over to Harrodsburg on a Saturday night just to satisfy her sweet tooth.

Humming Back Yesterday

Aberdeen Copeland was bringing yesterday back
from twenty years of hiding. Bringing it back in slow
motion. Never mattered where she was, what she was
doing—weeding the garden, shopping in the corner store,
making love to her Clovis, cooking beets, kneading bread
dough—it could come anytime.

She was stirring the soup beans, beginning to wash
the dishes when it hit. The water was hot, stinging her arms
clean up to the elbows. It just came over her again. Came
back in still life. A camera taking pictures.

Click. A teenaged Aberdeen in a purple wrap-around
dress with little green flowers. A toothy smile. Hair wild
and bushy like they wore it in the seventies. Wire hoop
earrings. A white sweater, knitted in big open loops, draped

around her shoulders. Pearl buttons down the front. Her hip jutted to one side. Her head cocked. Hands on waist. Flat stomach. Beaucoup lipstick. Dark pink.

Click. Mama comes in full view. Tall, big-boned, big-breasted. Shapely. Flawless makeup. Blue eye shadow. Long lashes. Black orchid lipstick. Mouth open. Laughing up some storm. One arm hidden in back of Tommy. The other hand resting on the kitchen counter in the house they used to live in up on Hustonville Street. Tommy is a foot shorter than Mama. His head is right at her shoulders. His spats shiny. Hair slicked back, a skunk streak running through the middle, just a little off to the side. His belly round as a balloon. White starched shirt. Black dress pants, held up by suspenders. No smile. No tie. A cigarette dangling from his lips. One of his big hands snaking around Mama's waist. Fingers big as hot dogs. His other hand spread out on the edge of the sink. His wedding band shining.

Click. God's Witness church over in Turnersville. Brother Smith up in the pulpit. Black robe. Wrinkled chin. His fist frozen in mid-air. Tommy's hand is under the coat spread out across Mama's lap.

The humming takes over. Back in her kitchen, Aberdeen is holding her head in her hands. Eyes closed. Elbows on the table. Legs gaped open.

Hum. Tommy's hand is under the coat, his hot-dog-fingered hand moving in some hidden place above Mama's thigh. Aberdeen is watching, though trying not to. She is old enough to know. And old enough to know better. *Hum.*

Brother Smith is sweating. He wipes his brow with a great big white handkerchief. His mouth is moving but there are no words. His arms are moving. Mama's legs are apart. She is moving like shouting. Nobody else notices. Aberdeen watches her head roll back. The coat is moving. Tommy turns his head. Grins at Aberdeen. She turns away but is drawn back.

"Aberdeen," Clovis starts off, "Aberdeen, you got the headache again?" He steps up behind her, places his hands on her shoulders and rubs. He smells of blood and death from the slaughterhouse. A smell that Aberdeen got used to a long time ago, but today it sits in her nose, makes her head swim. Clovis kisses her bent-over head.

"Yeah," she says, coming on back to this side of the world, "Clovis, you remember when Mama was with Tommy? Back when we was living up on Hustonville?"

"No baby," Clovis says, leaning over to kiss Aberdeen's neck, "that was before I knew y'all. Before we met. I still lived out Boneyville, remember? Need some aspirin? The doctor said plain aspirin was fine."

"Yeah," Aberdeen raises her head, answers only one of his questions, rubs the base of her neck, "yeah, could you get me some, honey?"

Aberdeen pulls all the pieces of herself back together. "Clovis, I'm awright," she yells in the bathroom direction. "Why don't you go head and take your shower, baby? I'm gonna finish supper."

The sound of running water puts calm in Aberdeen's kitchen. She wishes the past would stay past. Rubs the chill bumps off her arm. Rubs her belly.

By the time Clovis reaches singing stage in the shower, Aberdeen is back at the sink. Dishes washed. She peels Irish potatoes. Discards the peelings in old newspaper. Puts the fresh white potatoes in a pan of cold water. Watches them bob up, gleaming like hard-boiled eggs. From the window she can see her garden spot all covered by winter's brown. Come spring she will give it life again.

Aberdeen quarters the potatoes then halves the quarters. She stirs the beans. Drops the potato pieces in a skillet of hot grease. Pulls the milk from the icebox, reaches up, pulls cornmeal from the cabinet to start her hoecakes. Aberdeen, determined to win this fight, keeps on cooking. *Hum.* She turns the potatoes in the grease. Pours the cornbread batter into a cast-iron skillet, making little pancake circles. She slices yellow onion on a saucer. *Hum.* Pulls corn from the deep freezer. Plops the frozen lump into the saucepan. Cuts half a stick of butter into it. Frozen straight from the garden. Better than store-bought any day.

Hum. "Bitch, you don't know how to cook. Look at this damn cornbread. You call this shit cornbread?" Back on Hustonville Tommy has his thick fingers squeezing both sides of Mama's cheeks. Her face is squeezed together like a fish's mouth painted with black orchid lipstick.

*

Aberdeen stirs the beans. Flips the cornbread. Tastes the corn.

Hum. Tommy's two sheets to the wind. Liquor on his breath. In his other hand is the piece of cornbread all crumbled in his fist. Tommy eases off a little to see what Mama's got to say. "Aberdeen made it, sweetheart. It's her first time. That's all. You calm down, sugah, and I'll fix some more. Hear?" Mama tries to smile. Tommy gives her fish lips again.

Aberdeen sets the table, trying to sing over the humming in her head. A plate for her. One for Clovis.

51

Hum. Tommy's face is all tore up. Mama reaches over under the table between Tommy's legs. His face changes. He eases his hot-dog fingers. Rubs them across her face. Pulls Mama's face up close.

Knives, forks, jelly glasses. Ice.

Hum. Kisses her lips. Aberdeen sees his tongue flitting like a snake in and out of Mama's mouth. "Shhh," Tommy says at the end of the kiss, "it's just her first time." He laughs. "Shhh." He puts his big finger up to Mama's mouth making the hushing sign. Mama laughs. Rubs between his legs some more.

Aberdeen pours the sweet iced tea. Cuts a lemon up in it. Tears off paper towel for napkins.

Hum. Tommy slobbers on Mama's neck. Leaves spit running. Whispers something in her ear. Drags her laughing like a child to the back room.

Aberdeen puts bowls out for the beans.

    Hum. The table is set. Food's still hot. Aberdeen tries to eat her dinner. Tries to ignore the thumping sounds.

    Sits the lemon pie out for dessert. "Hmm," Clovis walks into the kitchen, rubbing his wet hair with a towel, smelling like Old Spice aftershave. His blue terrycloth robe pulled tight at his waist. "Baby, I needed that like you wouldn't believe. Feel good now. Your head still hurtin? You awright?"

    Aberdeen is at the counter, pouring the soup beans in a big serving dish.

    "Aberdeen?"

    She lines a bread basket with paper towels and puts the hoecakes in. Puts the fried potatoes in the big green bowl

Mama passed on to her. Notices the white chips around the edges. Notices how big the opening is.

"Aberdeen?" Clovis moves toward Aberdeen who is somewhere down in the green bowl.

"Huh? Clovis, you say something, baby?" She sticks in serving spoons and moves around him to put the food on the table. Sets out a jar of homemade relish. Rubs her belly.

"Think I need to call the doctor?" Clovis puts a worried look on his face.

"Naw, I'm fine."

"You shore?"

"I'm fine, Clovis. You hungry? Let's eat."

Clovis eyes Aberdeen and goes to town on his supper. Aberdeen watches her man eating what her hands have prepared. Taking up supper in big forkfuls. She smiles. Between bean, bread and potato, she tries to get a word in.

"Clovis, we gonna have a garden this year?" she starts, then keeps talking like it wasn't a question he was really supposed to answer. "I was thinking that we could plant some sunflowers out by the fence row." She takes a bite of beans. Chews. Talks. "How about some morning glories? You know Mama had morning glories all over the backyard up on Hustonville? Had yellow lilies all along the front walk. They always bloomed by Easter and . . ." Aberdeen feels the humming coming on and changes the subject. "Sugah, you have a good day? Seems like you tired."

Clovis is chewing as fast as he can, trying not to talk with his mouth full. Sips from his iced tea to help it all go down. Wipes the side of his mouth with the paper towel.

"Looks like we gonna need plenty of potatoes if nothing else," Aberdeen smiles. "Every time your elbow bends your mouth flies open. You'll be looking like me fore long." She pats her belly.

Clovis frees his full jaws. Laughs. Sips more tea. "Baby, you better go on and eat now, 'fore there ain't none left."

Aberdeen leans over to her husband. Rubs his arm. "You go on. There's plenty."

"My day was awright, baby. Same ole, same ole. Givens says he don't mind if I take some time off from the slaughterhouse. Did I tell you that?"

Aberdeen shakes her head, no. Gets up to cut the lemon pie. The knife goes in easy. She lifts the pie out with her fingers. Licks the sweetness off the tips.

54

"Baby, I don't know," Clovis shakes his head as she places it in front of him. "This might be too much. I'm awready bout to bust."

Aberdeen leaves the pie on the table to tease Clovis. Winks at him. Stands behind his chair and runs her fingers through his wet hair. She bends over to smell the clean shampoo scent. Clovis's head falls back onto her belly. Her hands reach out to his shoulders. She rubs. Trying to take the slaughterhouse up outta his muscles.

"Hmm, you put a man to sleep," Clovis says, his brown eyes shut. Aberdeen bends down and kisses him on the lips. Clovis reaches up and holds her there.

*

Click. Bobby Johnson. Aberdeen's first love. Bib overalls. Barefoot. Down by the creamery. It is a young kiss. A fresh kiss. Lips smooth like butter. Bobby reaches up her skirt. Reaches inside her panties. His face like agony. Begging.

Aberdeen holds on to Clovis. Lets him kiss her long.

"Love you, baby," he says, raising his head up and digging into the lemon pie. He puts the fork up to Aberdeen's mouth.

She takes a bite. Chews.

*   *   *

Way up in the night Clovis is sleeping, Aberdeen is tossing and turning trying to find a comfortable spot. Her dreams roll up like a reel-to-reel across her closed eyes.

She is running
up Hustonville
in a night fog.
Being chased.
Her heart is beating fast.
She hears Tommy's laugh,
in between houses,
cross the yards,
from the trees.
There is something,
someone,

at the end of the road
that she must get to
before Tommy.
The fog grows thicker.
The closer she gets
the farther away the something or someone moves.
There is no end to Hustonville Street.
Tommy is on her heels.
She can hear his breathing. Through the fog she sees arms
stretched out to her. Somebody crying. Screaming.
She can't make out a face. Tommy is still laughing, gaining
ground.

Aberdeen wakes up in a sweat. Sits straight up in the bed.
Clovis wakes up too.

"Baby . . . Baby, what in the world?"

"Nightmare," she says trembling through some tears.

Clovis takes her in his arms, pulls her head to his
chest.

"Shh," he says, "shh."

Before morning shines through the window, Aberdeen pulls herself from her safe place in Clovis's arms. Makes her way to the bathroom in a quiet way to let Clovis get his rest. Before she even gets to the toilet, Aberdeen feels a warm trickling down her leg and a slight shift in her belly.

*

Hum. Tommy steps through the brush. Grabs Bobby John-son by the shirt collar. Punches him in the mouth. "You better git, you little bastard." Bobby runs.

Aberdeen is frozen in the bathroom. The green tiles are wet around her feet.

Hum. Tommy grabs her by the shoulders. "You little fast tail whore." He commences to shaking her hard. Aberdeen cries. Bobby Johnson runs. "Nothing but a whore." Tommy slaps her face. Aberdeen pees her panties.

"Clovis! Lord have mercy. Clovis!"

57

    Clovis is out of bed and by her side. He takes her by the arm. Leads her into the bedroom.

Tommy has his hand around the meat just above her elbow. Jerking hard.

Clovis sets her on the bed. He washes her face with a warm rag, removes her gown. He washes her up and puts on her clothes.

*

Hum. Tommy takes her up the road, where his car is parked.

Clovis puts her into the car. In the car, Aberdeen is rocking back and forth in her seat. "Lord have mercy," she says over and over. "Shh," Clovis says, "baby, it's gonna be awright."

Hum. "Shut up." Tommy drags Aberdeen in the house. Yells for Mama but she's still at work. "Ain't no daughter of mine gonna be no slut." Tommy slaps her again. "You gonna be a whore, you gonna be treated just like one."

58   Aberdeen feels sharp pain up and down her back. "Lord have mercy." Clovis reaches over, pats her arm. "Hold on, baby."

The bed is cold. Smells like bleach. Clovis is by her side. Pain hits.

Tommy takes his hot-dog finger and jabs it between her legs. "This what you want? This what you want?" Pain.

Pain.

*

"No it was the first time . . ."

Pain. Clovis is by her side. Wiping sweat off her forehead. "This is her first time."

Hum. "It's her first time." Tommy laughs. There is a second finger poking away at her insides. "Lord have mercy." Pain. Tommy is laughing and jabbing. Laughing and jabbing.

Pain. Aberdeen clinches her teeth. Bears down.

Click. Tommy looks old. Thin. Dying. His hot-dog fingers shriveled. A cane between his legs. His eyes are yellow. Sad. Mama is dressed in black, practicing being a widow. Hair pulled back. Her shoulders drooped. Worn down. Worn out. No smile. No laugh.

Clovis is purring in her face. "Take it easy, baby we gonna be awright. We gonna be awright. You ready?" Clovis holds the baby up for her to see. Aberdeen holds the girl child in her arms. The baby's face is that of a moon. Bright. Round. Clovis leans down, kisses Aberdeen's lips. Kisses the baby's head. Aberdeen smiles, says, "You happy Clovis?"

Adds, "Me too" before he has a chance to answer. Tries to look forward to tomorrow. Tries to keep yesterday from humming back.

Peace of Mind

I am sitting here on vacation in my own damn house on a Saturday afternoon trying to have peace of mind. All three of my boys gone to summer camp. No man. Even the cat knows to leave me alone. I fix me a glass of lemonade, crack up laughing cause I done caught myself waiting for somebody to say, "Mama, can I have some?" and ain't nobody here to do that. Bout time I pop me some extra-butter microwave popcorn, lay down across my made-up bed, in my clean bedroom, quiet as a mouse, and open up my very own copy of A.J. Verdelle's *The Good Negress*, the phone rings.

Peaches is on the other end of line talking 'bout, "Who should I take to P.G. and Frieda's party?" And I'm saying, "Girl please," cause I can't even believe she's got the nerve to go, cause she knows and I know she's been sleeping with P.G. behind Frieda's back. And I guess that's what Frieda gets for bragging 'bout how good P.G. is up under some covers.

"Why shouldn't I go? Frieda invited me."

"Girl that is triflin' and I can't even believe . . . I wouldn't even have the nerve."

"Well that's what P.G. gets. I waited all night long for that muthafucka. He said he was gonna sneak away last night and he never did come. I wasted all that candlelight dinner and perfume and shit and he didn't even show."

"Peaches, now you know better. Why you tryin to play game, like he would really choose his part-time piece a ass over his full-time wife?"

"Well he don't seem to have no problem beggin for this ass when he's over here. And I have to tell you I be beggin back. Girl that man can give . . ."

"Peaches, please, I don't even want to be that deep in your business . . ."

"Well I think I'm gonna take Fred with me to the party. So P.G. can see that I ain't sprung over him, for real . . ."

"Hold on a minute."

I click over and I'm glad somebody's calling me so that I can get away from this trifling conversation. Peaches *is* trifling even if she has been my best friend since college.

"Ma-ma, make Danny 'em stop fightin before the camp people sends us home." Eric Jr sounds tore up with his brothers. I talk to my baby like Peaches ain't on the other line. I'm hoping she hangs up.

"Put Danny on the phone."

"Mama, I wasn't even doin nothin, see, dang. This boy tried to take one of my pancakes and you know how much I like pancakes, right, and then he tried to blame it on Duwon cause he didn't know Duwon was my brother, right, so, Duwon got on one side and I got on the other side, right, and we both hit him in his shoulders and gave him a charley horse then he wants to be runnin and tellin like some ole punk . . ."

"Boy, if you and Duwon don't behave yourselves, I'm beating y'alls' asses and you gonna be on punishment for the whole damn summer." And I look up to God praying that I don't have to enforce that one cause it would drive me crazy if them boys are in my house tearing up shit all summer long.

"I love you. Now put Duwon on the phone."

"Yes, ma'am."

"Mama, we wasn't even doin nothin, ole straight-up punk."

"Boy, if you and Danny don't behave you gonna be on punishment for the whole summer and you gonna get y'alls' asses whipped. Do you hear me boy?"

"Yes, ma'am."

"Dang, man I told you," I hear him put his hand over the phone and tell his brother. "She gonna make us stay all summer, dang."

"Duwon!"

"Yes, ma'am."

"Y'all better behave y'all selves. I love you. Now put Eric Jr back on the phone."

"Love you too, Mama. Bye."

"Hello."

"Eric Jr, since you the oldest, please try to keep your brothers in line for Mama. Okay. I'll pick y'all up next Sunday. You call me back if they keep cuttin up, hear. Love you. Bye."

"Okay. Bye, Mama."

Eric Jr don't sound pleased but he knows I mean what I said. The phone beeps again before I can hang up.

"Hello, Peaches."

"Hello, Sharon, it's me, Linda. I'm standing at your desk. I hate to bother you at home while you're on vacation and on a weekend too, but I'm working a little while today and can't find a file. I thought it might be on your desk somewhere. I just thought I would call you before we went rummaging through your desk to find it."

Dear Lord, I'm thinking to myself, they can't find a pimple on their ass when I'm not there, even with directions. And I don't know why she's sayin *we* when she knows ain't nobody crazy enough to work on a Saturday when they don't have to except her stupid, bouffant-haired, nose-up-Mr-Moore's-crack, ass.

"Hello. Hello, Sharon, are you there?"

I'm wishing I wasn't but I put my work voice on cause she is my supervisor.

"Yes, Linda," I say gritting my teeth, "that's fine, no problem. Which file is it that you are looking for?"

"The Chancery file," she says.

"The Chancery file is in my out-box on the right-hand

side of my computer. Didn't you get my memo telling you where everything was before I left?"

I'm thinking she just wants to be rummaging through my desk while I'm gone to see what she can find but at this very moment I really don't give a damn.

"Oh yes, I see it here. Sorry. I'm really sorry that I had to bother you during your vacation. Having a good time?"

"Oh yes, I sure am," I said chuckling being as fake as anything. "I'll see you next week. Uh-huh. Okay. You have a good weekend, too. Bye."

I lift my glass of lemonade and see that all my ice has melted and settle back into my book. I read a few pages and start to drift off. No phone. No kids. No Peaches. No job. Then the damn phone rings again.

"Hey, baby, it's me, Eric. The boys told me that they were goin to camp this week. I just thought you might be lonely and want to come and catch a movie or something. Maybe we could go over P.G.'s and Frieda's, I heard they havin a party. Whatchoo think?"

"What do I think? Eric, I think that we been divorced for two years and I am enjoying it that way and that every time the boys go off to camp or somewhere and you find out about it then you start worrying bout who I am spending my free time with and that it's none of your fucking business and send your goddamn child support, which is late by the way, before I haul your ass back into court and stop trying to come up with a way to get in my drawz cause it is not, I repeat, not, going to happen. That's what the fuck I think!"

I hang up on that muthafucka and just as soon as I do, I'll be damned if the phone does not ring again.

"Look muthafucka, I told you . . ."

"Girl, what in the world's wrong with you?"

It's Peaches again.

"Why you leave me hangin? I just went on and hung up and did my nails. I got this new polish you know, its purple, P.G. thinks it's sexy and Fred likes it too, so I can't lose. I thought you were my best friend. Now, my problem is gonna be what if Fred's busy or I can't get him to go. Then P.G.'s gonna think I'm home by myself waitin on him and I know he's gonna be home fuckin Frieda tonight after the party, cause that's how shit happens. And I want him to be thinkin bout me when he does it. And if he is gonna be with his wife then I'm gonna be gettin me some too with Fred or some goddamn body . . ."

I lay the phone on the bed and place a pillow over it and let her talk. Peaches faintly sounds like a mouse squeaking and squealing her heart out. I pick up my book and flip over the back. A.J. Verdelle's looking back at me, strength in her face, her dreads hanging down. I flip back to my page and start reading. I hear Peaches squeaking and I'm thinking Peaches need to quit thinking about a piece of man and be looking for peace of mind. I know I am.

Mr

Mr insisted that Fannie stay on those long
nights while his chalky wife lay dying under laced covers.
And even though Fannie wetted those death-blue lips with
herb tea, she knew it was Mr who needed healing most.
Tainted goodbye whispers as the sun crept in bringing brand
new. Most days dread weighed her down so heavy she could
hardly move. She had threatened to quit once while his
wife's eyes still sparkled green but Mr had begged her to
stay. Begged her husband, Jake, to let her stay. Said his wife
couldn't make it without her. But she always knew it was
he who couldn't make it. She always knew.

And Jake labored alone in the fields. Fields that would
never be his own. His wrinkled, dark hands too blessed
with dawn til dusk sun rubbed across his dusty brow with

only his thoughts for company. He wondered why his babies weren't brown.

It went okay most days til Mr's wife started ailing real bad. Her blue lips quivered, refused herb tea. And Jake held steady till the last baby came. Lil Star wasn't even dark about the ears, had those funny lookin eyes. But he loved her just the same as he did the seven others. But she never seemed quite right to him. Not like the others, bless her heart.

And that next season when Jake's mind got troubled, Fannie could see his mind turning in the field, with each pull of the plow. Fannie was doing her washing and nearly scrubbed the blood out of her hands pining over Jake's thinking. She wanted to comfort him in some way but words wouldn't come and the time for hugs had passed between them.

And when Mr disappeared that same night he laid his chalky wife down to rest Jake just sat on the back porch in the big wooden rocker and no longer went to the fields. He just smiled a quiet smile at Lil Star and sipped on a cool cup of well-water as she played make-believe in the dust and sun, turning black as the ace of spades.

Mine

Joe Scruggs stood firm on the notion that black women
do not get their breasts worked on. A white woman,
maybe, but not a sister. Add more on? Now that's something
even he would give the green light to. But definitely under
no circumstances does a sister ever take away what God has
blessed her with.

But there Racine was right in front of him. Crossing
the street at the corner of Main and Broadway. Heading
into Desha's Restaurant. Wearing a loose flowing bright
purple dress.

She had already cut off her long, straight hair, started
wearing it nappy, natural. She knew he liked it long. But
she cut it anyway. Next thing he knew she had left him
and married a brother from Philadelphia. Some kind of

professor up at the university. But to go and get her forty-four triple Ds whittled down was going too far. She must have really lost her natural mind. He heard about it. People talk. He always kept informed about his exes through the grapevine.

The moment he spotted her, he knew the word on the streets was true-fact. The grape fabric of her blouse was flowing where the fullness of forty-four triple Ds used to jiggle. His eyes followed his used-to-be across the street and watched her go inside. He could still see her through the window, just behind the large white *e-s-h* in the *Desha's* spelled out on the glass. She still stood out. The only black woman in sight. Wearing deep purple. A bright orange head-wrap around her head, her kinky hair peering out around the edges. He didn't like his women in loud colors. Brought on too much attention. Racine disappeared into the crowd. He wondered what her husband must think. *A sister getting whittled on. Shit.* The light changed to green. Joe could hear the faint roar of traffic moving. But he was stuck on Broadway. Couldn't seem to make the right-hand turn that would take him to Darlene's house, where he would spend another Saturday night.

He sat at the light thinking about following Racine inside. Wondered if the sight of him would cause a commotion. Wondered if somewhere deep down, some tiny part of her still wanted him. And this husband who allowed shit like this to happen? *What kind of a man is he?* Darlene was chattering away in the passenger's seat. *What are we gonna do this weekend, Joe Scruggs? What movie you wanna see? What about dinner? I got me a taste for some red beans and rice.* She called his name louder when he didn't answer. *Joe Scruggs, you listening? How about some beans and rice? Huh? My mama's recipe. Tomatoes in it and a touch of jalapeno.* Joe was somewhere between the sway of Racine's hips twisting into Desha's and the missing triple Ds he had grown so fond of. *I'll cook some cornbread, too.* He had spent many nights cuddled up with them. Racine became secondary at times. *Or do you want rolls? Mama always fixed it with cornbread but rolls sound good.* And now she had the nerve to get them cut on. Cutting up *his* finery like that. Maybe it was all for spite. *Cornbread or rolls?*

Darlene shook his arm and at the same time a horn honked. In the rearview mirror Joe could see the white man in the truck. His face all red and screwed up tight. His arms flying up in short, quick bursts. His mouth moving. Pounding a fat white fist on the steering wheel. The light changed from green back to red and Joe was still sitting in traffic, the brakes on his hatchback still pushed to the floor. A symphony of horns blowing behind him. *Joe Scruggs*— Darlene always called him by his whole name—*Joe Scruggs. You daydreaming again?* Two years now but she still called him like that. *Joe Scruggs.* Using his whole name. Drawing it out too long. Got on Joe's nerves sometime. Much of what Darlene did got on his nerves, at least *sometime.* There was something to be said about the chase. But after that, tedium had set in. He really didn't want *his* woman up under him all the time.

Joe had met Darlene at the drugstore, where she

worked part-time after her day job. He had found her bent over in the cosmetics department, retrieving make-up from a box, stocking the little steel poles on the shelves with packages of mascara and face powder. He had stood and watched the spread of her slacks across her backside as she bent over. Her braided extensions, looking like long, thin tree limbs blowing between the space between her legs. He made his way down aisle five so he could get a glimpse of her face. Grabbed some shaving cream off the shelf. *Excuse me, could you help me out here?* Darlene uprighted herself, throwing her extensions back like a white woman. Joe gave her the once-over. Not too much make-up. Cute in her own way. Nice breasts. Nice wide hips. Then he followed with a long story about him needing hypoallergenic shaving cream. By the end of the thirty-minute conversation, Joe left the store with the few items he came to get and Darlene's phone number and address neatly folded in his shirt pocket. He winked at her on his way out the door. *Joe Scruggs, right?*

In the beginning she had been hard, damn near impossible, to get. It took great skill for Joe to juggle Racine and chase Darlene at the same time. At first, all he ever got was Darlene's answering machine. Then, somewhere between their first dinner date and Racine catching them embraced in a slow drag on the American Legion dance floor, Darlene became predictable. He heard his phone ringing every day after work. Before he reached the top step of his apartment building and turned the key at 729, the incessant ringing began. A pause. Then ringing again. *Hey hon. Just got in the door. Can I call you back?* No need to inquire as to who was calling. He knew. *Joe Scruggs, how was your day?* Always the same. Phone calls every night at the same time. An occasional midweek meeting for dinner or lunch or sex. Weekends: Darlene's apartment, movie, dinner, sex. Always the same. But figuring out Racine was a real challenge. *How could she do this? It had to be spite.*

He glanced over at Darlene, who was sitting quietly now. Tired of being ignored. Mad. Looking out the car window. Her arms crossed. Her lips curled tight. *Sorry shug, what did you say?* Silence. Main Street turned into Leestown Road. Joe pulled his hatchback off onto the side street that led to Darlene's apartment. Two bedrooms. Deluxe cable. Plenty of room to spread out. Even a pool for the summer. Her cooking wasn't bad, either. Joe used his own key to open the door. Fanned his arm out like he was making an introduction of royalty. Motioned for Darlene to enter first. She had to laugh. He chipped the edge off her anger. Inside the entrance, Joe grabbed Darlene. Pulled her close. Pinned her against the backside of the closed door. There was no resistance. No remaining sign of her being mad. He kissed her. Up against her he could feel the bigness of her chest. *See. Black women do not get their breasts worked on.* He closed his eyes tight. But there she was again. Racine. In her grape outfit. Smiling. Laughing at him. Floating across his brain. Her breasts whittled down from the size of cantaloupes to grapefruit. *Just for spite.* He kissed Darlene hard and long. Hard and long. Until Racine, floating, spinning in all that purple disappeared. Later that night there would be no leaving the apartment for the usual Saturday night movie. After the red beans and rice and the late show on Channel 7, Joe whisked Darlene off to the bedroom. He fumbled in the dark like a nervous teenager for the clasp on the back of her bra. Sighed at the freed weight of her breasts. Cupped them in his hands. *Mine.*

Women's Secrets

Mama breathes heavy in her sleep next to me, the covers rising and falling. I nuzzle closer into the curve of her spine and smell her sweetness. Lanolin scented plaits tickle my nose.

I hear Grandpa Joe coming down the steps. His weight against the rickety steps sounds like he's gonna come crashing through. He coughs his old man's cough and spits phlegm and baccer juice out the back door. The tin buckets make clanging noises gainst the water table as he picks 'em up. Metal gainst metal sound echoes from wall to wall. He's headed to the well. After he's done pulling water he'll go over the hill near the smokehouse and follow the dirt path to the toilet. He always does.

The door creaks open.

Clack.

The screen door smacks the jamb. And I know Grandpa Joe's mouth is making white puffs of smoke in the brisk air as he crosses the yard.

Big Mama's slippered feet brush gainst the tacked rug as she makes sideways steps down the stairs. I know she has on her Wednesday housedress. The faded one with pink and yellah flowers and an unraveling hem running clean around the skirt tail looking like Indian fringe.

Two . . . three . . . four . . . six . . . seven.

She's on the last step now. The wood floor under the linoleum gives a little with each step as she makes way round her kitchen. The old time clock on the kitchen shelf strikes a baritone seven. I feel Mama moving beside me. Most time she's already up 'fore Big Mama comes downstairs. Today she's sleeping a long time.

"Shit," she says as she climbs over me, knocking half the cover off my feet. I still play possum, taking in the morning.

"Shit fire," Mama says in a loud whisper to herself. "Mama gonna be mad with me now."

I wriggle round covering my feet back up. Then I peep through a hole tween the sheet and my covers and see Mama pull down her drawers, take the top off the pot and pee. She pees so long I almost get mad cause if she pees too close to the top I'll have to empty the pot out the back door before I can use it or else go on outdoors. The thoughts of it gives me the shakes cause I'm cold enough right where I'm at.

Mama throws on her housedress, whisper-cussing her-self all the way. Big Mama is washing up her hands now. I hear the wash pan rocking back and forth. It's got bumps in it and don't sit square with the table no more. Mama's in the kitchen now making a big racket cause she thinks Big Mama's real mad at her. The skillet and biscuit pan hit together as she pulls them from the cupboard.

"Girl, you gonna wake that baby," Big Mama says. "And you best git yourself over here and wash your hands fore you lay them on somebody's food. What the world done got into you?"

"Yes, ma'm," I hear my mama say. "Sorry I got up so late."

Big Mama don't say nothing but I know she giving Mama one mean look. Somebody is sifting flour. The *pat, pat . . . pat, pat* of flour dough starts up and thinking bout biscuits makes me hungry.

"Ollie, you looking awful peeked and sleeping awful long," Big Mama says to Mama. "You in a family way again?"

Big Mama starts to say something else but it sounds like her words just get caught way down deep in her throat. She clears her throat, trying to get her words back up in her mouth and Mama don't say nothing.

"Lord, chile, ain't you learned nothing from the first time?" Big Mama starts back up but her words are trembling again and she stops talking.

I smell cured ham frying now. Its sweet smoky scent fills my nose. My belly's trying to tell me it's hungry but I ain't got no time to listen right now. My ear's bent toward other talk.

"I seen that Adams boy sniffing round here at your skirts but he ain't no count. Him nor his brother. His daddy weren't no count neither. What he gonna give a family, girl? Ain't never gonna be nothing. Ain't got no learning. Ain't gonna never have no land. Gambling and carrying on like sin."

I'm just wondering why Big Mama so upset bout ole Mr Adams for? Maybe cause he always bragging bout where he's been and don't seem to set on staying round here long. But he bought me and Mama new Easter dresses. And one time he gave me a bag of hard candy just for going over to Aunt Fannie's with Cousin Addie Bea. Said he wanted to spend time alone with Mama while Big Mama and Grandpa Joe were out of the house. I didn't mind one bit.

Yeah, I like Mr Adams with his slicked back hair and big black mustache. He's always trying to kiss me and tugs on my hair. Calls me Thickplait but I like him just the same. Mama seems to be stuck on him, too, and I like seeing my Mama happy. I just don't see the difference it makes if he don't have no learning, cause I don't like ciphering or reading none either. I side with Mr Adams any day on not wanting no schooling. Big Mama always fussing bout learning and getting educated. I don't see no sense in it. And I figure Grandpa Joe got enough land for us all. Sixty-some acres I heard Big Mama tell Aunt Fannie.

"Chile, mens these times just ain't like your daddy," Big Mama takes a big loud breath and starts in on Mama again. "Ain't nare one of 'em no more than breath and britches, specially them Adams boys. Watch my words now, girl. I'm telling you. Ain't good for not a damn. God in heaven forgive me but ain't good for not a damn. Breath and britches all they are."

Mama still don't say nothing.

"Honey, I know you get lonesome living way out here with nothing but your kin people round but them Adams boys been raised with city ways and don't mean country girls like you nothing but harm. I can just feel it. You mind my words.

"I was young once, too. Had urges. When your daddy was courting me, he had his work cut out. Yes Lord. I was a feisty tail, now. And could daaance. Couldn't nobody touch me."

Big Mama laughs loud remembering her young days. Then her voice drifts on back to serious.

"They just don't make 'em like Joe no more. Your daddy's a good man. But that boy, he just gonna keep on making his bed where he can—going pillar to post."

Mama commenced to crying real hard like she know Big Mama is right and everything is quiet cept Mama's crying. Big Mama don't say no more. She just let Mama cry it out for a long while. I pull my covers tight cause I'm wanting to run in and hug my Mama. My chest starts burning and I feel like crying too but I just grab up my covers and hush up. Tears run down my face quiet and hit my quilt, making little dark spots cross its patterns. Big Mama goes on talking and her and Mama don't know I'm awake.

"Chile, I know your heart's hurting but you can't make babies with first one then the other. Word'll get out that you used goods for sure. You got a precious heart, Ollie. I know you can give your babies all the loving you got but wait till you got something to give 'em sides love. They gonna need a might more than that."

Mama cries some more real low like and Big Mama's words sound like they under water. I 'spect they hugging each other up now. Voices stop in the kitchen again and all I'm hearing is cooking noises.

Grandpa Joe comes back in.

Clack.

The screen door shuts again then I hear the big door close.

"Shoo-wee it sure is getting chilly out there." Grandpa Joe makes a funny sound like a chill just ran clean through him. "Winter be here fore you know it. I'll have to put up the stove fore long."

"Morning ladies," he says to Mama and Big Mama real pleasant. The morning sun done filled him up, too.

"Morning," they say together like they back on the same side. I hear Grandpa Joe walk through the kitchen and settle hisself in the sitting room to wait on breakfast.

I lift the quilts up off me and roll out the bed. My gown falls down past my hips to its proper place. The ruffle swirls, rests right above my ankles. I been wearing this same ole gown since Big Mama bought it from some peddler man two Christmases ago. I sure need the new one Aunt Fannie promised to make me. Shoo-wee, my feet are cold.

I find yesterday's socks beside my shoes and slip 'em on.
They some rank but all I want is to be warm.

Making out like I just woke up, I walk through the
house yawning and carrying on. The coal and wood stove
stands cold over in the corner of the sitting room, still
covered by a big, blue skirt. I try to imagine heat coming
from it for a few minutes but lose the thought quick.

"Bout time you got up, girl," Grandpa Joe says grinning his wide-mouthed grin with no teeth. "You gonna
sleep your life away."

"Good morning, Grandpa Joe," I whisper in my pretend sleepy voice and kiss him on his cheek. He's got prickly,
white whiskers growing up out of his copper face and they
scratch me.

"These ole whiskers gonna bite cha," he says and
jumps at me from his rocking chair. I laugh real loud and
run on in the kitchen.

"Good morning, baby," Big Mama says as she beats
eggs up foamy with a wire whisk. She wraps her free arm
around me tight. "You awful loud for a lazy girl what just
rolled out the bed."

"Hmmm," I yawn and kiss her jaw.

"You sure are a lazy little girl," she says, giving me
the eye. "It's almost lunch time now." She laughs and I
move closer to Mama.

"Morning, Mama."

"Morning, Sugar Lumpkin," she says back, freeing
both her hands long enough to wipe them on her apron
and squeeze me up tight.

I search Mama's big brown eyes for a sign of tears and kiss her right on the lips. The tears are gone now but the sorrow still there. Big Mama and Mama move round the kitchen like they dancing. Eggs sizzle in ham drippings and thicken white at the edges. Apples stirred, biscuits checked on. I just move out the way and watch.

The whistling pot sings. Steam fogs up the windows and makes the air white. I pick up a washing pan and Mama pours streams of clear, hot water into the metal pan. Steam rises onto my face warming me up. I walk back to me and Mama's room, watching myself cause I sure know what a single drop of hot water feels like on a bare arm or toe. Grandpa Joe don't mess with me as I walk through the sitting room cause he don't want me to burn myself.

While the water is cooling off, I get my gown off real slow and hold my rank socks up with my fingertips and let them drop to the floor. Me and Addie Bea stomped in the creek yesterday as we was going up to Aunt Fannie's place. And I wore wet socks all day so as Big Mama wouldn't know. She's always saying the creek has a beauty to be feared. She says that water has been known to draw a body in and drown a person.

I lift up the pot top and I'm glad Mama didn't pee clean up to the edge. I'm shivering but I don't see no steam coming up off my fresh pee and figure it must not be too cold. I bounce my privates dry over the pot and put the top back.

The mirror on the dresser is fogged up. Water beads from my wash rag drops onto the wood. I wipe it up real quick cause Big Mama don't want her furniture ruint. I rub lye soap cross my wash rag and wash my face, up and down my sides and 'cross my hind end. I look in the mirror and think to myself how one day I'm gonna fill out pretty like Mama. And a nice man like Mr Adams gonna come courting me. I wash good up under my arms so Big Mama won't say I smell like onions, wash 'tween my privates a long while and wonder what it feels like to be in a family way.

"Iola Jean," Grandpa Joe hollers from the kitchen.

"Sir?" I say almost spilling my washing pan.

"Food's going to waste in here."

"I'm coming," I holler back.

I dry off quick and slip into my drawers, shirt and denims. By the time I get clean socks, put on my shoes and throw my wash water out the back door, Grandpa Joe bout to say grace.

"God bless this food here that's meant for everybody. For Christ's sake. Amen."

The red-eye gravy is running off my ham and heading for my biscuit. I grab it up quick cause I don't like wet biscuits. Wet biscuits bring slop to mind for me. Fried apples sliding in butter head toward my eggs and I make little dams all over my plate so nothing touches fore I start eating.

We all eat silently cept for Mama or Big Mama saying, "Want some more?" every little while me and Grandpa Joe nodding or saying, "yeah" or "no". Course I don't say "yeah" or "no", just Grandpa Joe. I say "yes ma'am" and "no ma'am" like I'm sposed to.

Big Mama and Mama stop eating ever so often and fill up me and Grandpa Joe's milk glasses, give us second helpings. Mama don't eat much though. She just takes a couple of bites off her ham and makes little circles in her eggs with a fork. She and Big Mama just keep trading looks back and forth cross the table like they still talking in the quiet. Back and forth. Back and forth. Til Grandpa says, "Y'all sure awful quiet in here this morning."

Grandpa just looks from Big Mama to Mama to me and shakes his head cause nobody says nothing. I look at Mama and Big Mama looking at each other again and all us women just hold our tongues and keep our secrets.

Tipping the Scales

Josephine Childs was a big woman. She stood up around five foot eleven and weighed round two hundred and fifty pounds. She wasn't sloppy fat though, just big, solid. Anybody who thinks big women can't get no man just needs to sit down and chat with Josephine. She's sure had her hands full in the men department most all her life. Josephine came into this world on the edge of a storm and them rain clouds followed her round for years. And all Josephine's children was brought in the world pretty much under the same circumstances that she was born into. Miss Ethel Childs, Josephine's mama, was sneaking round with Edgar Walls, a mortician that traveled handling the black folks' dead kin in about three or four little towns clumped together, when she came up with the bun in the oven what turned out to be Josephine. Edgar was already married and had three full grown children back over in a town called Middleburg when Miss Ethel gave him the news. He built Miss Ethel a house right outside of Stanford, where she lived for her to raise Josephine in as long as she never said a word about him being the daddy.

Now in them times having a baby outta wedlock carried more seriousness than it does today. The whole town bout tipped over with everybody traveling to the edge of it to see what Ethel Childs was a-doing. Lotta folks went to they grave worrying and fretting cause they couldn't crack into Miss Ethel's business. Course Edgar snuck in and out of that house for years seeing Miss Ethel and Josephine on up until he died without a soul knowing it. Even said he loved them but just never had the with-it-all to leave his wife. Miss Ethel died when Josephine was twenty-five and she set up housekeeping just like her mama.

Josephine started having babies to have something for herself. Her mama always belonged to her daddy and her daddy was somebody else's husband and somebody else's daddy most of the time, which didn't leave much for her. Now as far as why she was hell bent on having men that always belonged to somebody else, I guess that's all she had ever known or maybe all she thought she deserved.

Her first child, Clifford, was by a man down in Calvary who was engaged to be married. His name was Cleavon, I think, well don't matter too much what his name is now. He met Josephine down at The Brown Diner, that's where she's worked all these years as a waitress, from six in the morning to two in the evening most every week day. Cleavon, or whatever his name was, was in town with the state people, building the new highway. He and the rest of the highway makers came into The Brown bout everyday for lunch for a month. Josephine was eyeing him so he started eyeing her back. They had made waitress to customer conversation, you know the kind all waitresses make just to make sure they get a tip. So Josephine already knew most of the man's business. She knew he was from up Calvary. Knew he was engaged and how much he loved his wife-to-be. But she just kept on making eyes at him and then toward the end of the month when they was getting ready to finish off the highway, she wore a real low-cut dress to The Brown, not exactly the kinda outfit that a woman should be waitressing in but Josephine knew what she was doing. When she practically laid her big double-D breasts out on the man's plate it was more than he could handle, wife-to-be and all. So Josephine scribbled her address on a napkin and Cleavon made his way to the edge of town for a visit. Now I'm sure it sounds strange to you but Josephine was twenty-five and her mama had just died and she hadn't never had no man. She tried to tell Cleavon that when he mounted hisself up on top of her, slurping, hungry for them big double-Ds he had seen a peek of. But he had left all his tenderness back in Calvary with his wife-to-be and wall-ered all over her real rough-like. I guess like a man whose told a woman he's engaged to be married and she keeps on after him anyway. Josephine cried at the pain in her body and the pain in her heart. Cleavon went on out the door, packed his bags and left even before the highway was made. He had made enough in Stanford, I guess. All that wallering, mean-style, had made Clifford. When Josephine got her belly full, the town bout tipped over again with all the folks bending their ear toward her door to try and find out her business. Didn't nobody know nothing but the highway makers and by the time Clifford was bout to come they was long gone. Word through the town was that she was her mama made over. The Browns what owned the diner didn't fire her though. They knowed she needed the money with a brand new baby. Josephine kept on waitressing til she couldn't stand no more, had the baby and came on back to work in four or five weeks just as soon as she got her baby with a sitter.

Josephine's milk barely had time to dry fore she was back at it again. Same story. She hooked herself up with some businessman in a suit that grounded hisself for a week on his way to Tennessee. Couldn't even tell you his name, cause I couldn't pronounce it when he was here. He sure was a good-looking something though. A flashy man glittering and flittering round like gold. Rings on most his fingers. Always running his hand through his slickered back hair. Didn't look like no black man we'd ever saw, though he claimed he was. By Wednesday of the week he stayed, he had moved on in with Josephine. He was a gentle lover and although he didn't have no love in his heart for the woman, he didn't want to leave no woman he had breezed through on this earth to ever say he didn't do nothing for em. To him, love making was an art. Josephine's body was a canvas and he was the brush, painting her up one side and down the other til she fell off to sleep. Now why Josephine got all teary eyed when he left, I don't know, cause she knew he was just passing through on his way from here to there, but she shed tears anyway. He took her into town on Saturday night, draped across his arm. They danced to the juke box in The Brown in front of everybody. He kissed her full on the lips and all the women in the restaurant sucked in air. He took her home, painted his most breathtaking picture and come morning he was a breeze in the wind. That breeze left behind Goldean nine months later, a beautiful girl child indeed.

Don't get me wrong, now. Mixed round among all this cavorting, Josephine was a good mama. She always had them babies shining—took them to church, even with all the stares—and hurried home to them every night after she got off at The Brown.

After the one's name I can't pronounce, Josephine settled down a bit. Men would shoot her feisty looks and she wouldn't take them up and all kinds of men came through The Brown traveling down the new highway but she didn't give none of them the time of day. I guess it was two or three years til she got up with Jewell Barker and started shaking his tree behind a closed door.

Jewell Barker was a married man and to make things worse he lived right in Stanford. Josephine saw him and his wife, Maylene, every Sunday in church. She eyed them often, not cause she was after Jewell, but because she was envious of the love they seemed to share. He always had his hand at his wife's waist or she would notice Maylene pat his knee. But all that changed when Josephine's washer went out. Mrs Brown down at the diner told her to call Jewell Barker cause he owned a fix-it business and could fix most anything. And I guess he could. He went up to Josephine's house three times with four different parts for that washer and by the fourth time he had fixed it all, including Josephine. At first Josephine wasn't paying Jewell no mind at all. She hummed herself through her evening chores, cooking supper, reading a bedtime story and putting the kids to bed. Every night, after she put the kids to bed was her time, she let her hair fall down round her shoulders and put on a long purple housecoat that come down to the floor. The first night Jewell had seen her in the doorway, her hair all down hitting against that purple, he was hooked. It just took her a little longer to get hooked on him. In fact, she thought Jewell wasn't much a man at all to look at. He was a lot shorter than her, a small man, and talked real quiet and stuffy-nosed like. The only thing she saw in him was his gentleness with his wife.

"Josephine, I'm sorry to have to bother you again, but I'm gone have to come back tomorrow evening with another part," he said his voice a whining and wheezing. That was on the third day.

"Seems like I ain't never gonna get to wash up all these clothes. Now is this thing gonna work again or not Jewell, am I gonna have to get another one? How much is this costing me?" she snapped back, her hands on her hips.

"Don't worry Josephine," he said back, "I promise

you I won't charge you anymore for the labor just the parts."

After he got her mind at ease bout the finance of it all, he got to working on her steady.

"All of us at the church was real sorry to see Miss Ethel go a few years back."

Josephine knew he was lying cause didn't nobody in town like her mama, but just that he was trying softened her heart a little.

"Yeah, I still miss mama like it was yesterday. Have some coffee, Jewell?"

They sat awhile at the kitchen table, her getting a chance that she didn't get too often to talk about the goodness of her mama, him soaking in all the joy she had in her that she don't show to nobody. They talked way up til the morning. Jewell rubbed his hand cross her face and left. He told Maylene that he got an emergency call over in the next county and had been up all night, fixing a furnace trying to keep somebody's young-uns from freezing to death.

The next time Jewell came through Josephine's door the spare part sat on top the washer and they talked some more. He even played with Clifford and Goldean before they was put down for bed. After the kids was asleep, Jewell worked his way from his side of the couch down to Josephine's, before she knew it, like men do. He ran his hand through her hair and around the back of her neck and pulled her down to him. She didn't even attempt to resist. He kissed her long and slow, a soft kiss, til they was both in the world they had made. He kissed her neck and put his arms around her as far as they could reach. "Jewell don't you think you need to be heading on home," formed in her brain to say but the words got lost in the kindness of Jewell Barker's eyes. She tried to think bout all them things she knew to be true. He's married. He's short and little. His voice always sounds like he's full a cold. But before too long she had grabbed Jewell by the hand and led him down the hall to her bedroom. When they laid longways so the right parts were meeting, Jewell's head rested right at Josephine's breasts and his feet hit at somewhere up round her shins but none of that mattered. Jewell kissed her breasts like they were her lips and Josephine moved Jewell around on top of her where she wanted him to go. It felt nice to her to be in charge of a man, even under these circumstances. Jewell kept lying to his wife, coming by Josephine's, fixing things two or three times a week, Josephine a throwing him all over that bed, and they both getting just what they needed out of it. I guess it took two or three months fore Josephine's monthly stopped again. Jewell quit coming by in the late months but started back up again after Steve Edward was born. Things wasn't the same at first but soon they fell into a pattern. Jewell came by on Mondays and Wednesdays and dropped off a little money and stayed a little while. Just long enough for the kids to get to sleep and to let Josephine throw him around on the bed, if she wanted to.

Josephine was still working at The Brown but the Browns like everybody else in town was starting to look at her even more funny. They let her stay though cause she needed the money. Three kids now by three different daddies. Two of them a mystery and a third by a breeze in the wind that had a name couldn't nobody pronounce. Things was getting kinda rough for Josephine with four mouths to feed now including her own. The money that Jewell was dropping off and her wages at The Brown together wasn't enough to keep up with the bills. Course her house was paid off, her daddy had took care of that, but there was still the lights, water and gas and all not counting the phone, groceries and her climbing day-care bill. So when George Elvis started sniffing round The Brown after her, flashing wadsa money he done won shooting craps, it wasn't hard deciding what to do. Josephine took up with George Elvis quick. He was tall, taller than her. Stood about six-four, slim, a light-skinned man. Bits of gray sprinkled all through his hair, even though he was round the same age as her. George was the kind of man that took up a whole room when he walked in it no matter how big it was. And when he walked in The Brown flashing money and set his sights on Josephine, he swept her on up with the rest of the room without anyone knowing but just them two. George Elvis was known in town as a ladies' man. Was all time juggling two, three women at a time and Josephine knew it. But in no time he was out at her house ringing her doorbell at midnight after his Friday night crap shooting. First time he came wasn't no games played. He walked straight on in her house like he owned it, laid two hundred dollars out on the table in a fan and said to her with matter-of-fact in his voice, "Here is some money for you and your babies like I promised, now how bout showing some appreciation to ole George Elvis." He walked round Josephine like a cougar stalking deer meat and came up on her from behind rubbing all he had up next to her. She could smell beer and cigarettes stale on his breath but it was nice to have a take-charge man again. And charge he took. Josephine was so used to Jewell's kind of loving that when George Elvis flipped her cross the bed she was kind of shook up at first til she felt his tongue moving, beer, cigarettes and all, round in her mouth. George Elvis made love to her strong and good and would never stop for nothing til she said his name.

Mondays and Wednesdays still belonged to Jewell and Fridays was George Elvis's. They all three had an agreement. George Elvis agreed to do whatever the hell he wanted and come see her on Friday nights after his crap shoot. She kept her Fridays clear and he kept the money coming in. He didn't even know that Jewell Barker was the other man and really didn't care. He had more women than enough. And Jewell Barker agreed that long as he dropped by twice a week or so and let Josephine throw him around on the bed, the way she had when they was making her third child, then he didn't have to worry about his wife, Maylene, finding out or make no real child support payments. Josephine just agreed to do whatever it took to keep both her men happy and be able to feed her children, pay her bills and grab a piece of happiness for herself now and then.

The problem with all this was that Josephine's pieces

of happiness was getting smaller and smaller all the time. Her kids were getting older and she wanted to give them something sides a Monday/Wednesday daddy. And she wanted more than a Monday/Wednesday/Friday man. She would see Jewell and Maylene in church every Sunday and long for what they had. Course he played Maylene like a fiddle, but she wasn't talking bout that part. Jewell didn't hold her at the waist like he did Maylene. Not that she wanted Jewell to be the one doing the holding. It's that she wanted somebody to really love her all out in the open like that. Most time now when Jewell made his trip over, Josephine would just sit and stare at the floor. Jewell would motion his head toward the bedroom and she would shake her head, no, and he would go on home to Maylene. And George Elvis was one of them men that didn't see love in no woman. Just saw a contest. Saw making love kinda like setting a record. He worked and sweated and poked, kissed, prodded, rubbed . . . whatever he had to do to please a woman and when he got done and she called out his name, he was ready to go find the next one. Josephine got to the point where she got to moaning and groaning on George Elvis soon as he got started, just to get him out the door quick.

She went to spending more time with her kids. She let 'em stay up later cause there wasn't no need in rushing them off to bed. Sometimes they was all up playing when George Elvis would come over on Friday nights. He would leave and Josephine was glad that he did. Only thing that bothered her was the money part and she figured she'd find a way.

Jewell started just coming by on just Mondays and

when he came, he'd come early and spend most all his time playing with the kids, specially Steve Edward.

Josephine started working overtime at The Brown on weekends to try and make ends. And I guess it was a good thing cause if she didn't, she never would have met Ashe Yerby. Ashe Yerby was a broad-chested, stout, long, brown-skinned man with a voice so deep a body could fall right in it. He worked for the sewing factory and had got transferred from way down in Alabama to the Stanford plant. He came by bus one Saturday morning and stopped at The Brown for a bite of breakfast. Josephine served Ashe without a notice, filling his coffee cup, giving him some more eggs and gathering up her tip when he left. Ashe returned for lunch and set at the same table. He asked Josephine directions to an apartment he'd called about. Words danced out his mouth like thunder and Josephine didn't even notice. She scribbled directions on a wet napkin and kept on going.

"Ashe Yerby, I'm moving here to y'alls town," he says extending his hand out toward Josephine. "I'm new to round here. New to Kentucky."

"JosephineChildsWelcometoStanfordWelcometo KentuckyWannahearthespecials?" she said shifting from one of her hips to the other trying to get some relief down to her feet. She ignored his outstretched hand.

"Okay, let's hear em," Ashe said, trying to smile through Josephine's sadness.

"Yourchoicefriedchickenordeepfriedshrimpwithcoleslaw frenchfriescornbreaddessertanddrinkfourninetyfive," Josephine said like a menu-machine. No smile, no nothing.

Ashe ordered the special and watched Josephine work.

He moved in his new apartment so he got to cooking for hisself and didn't go to The Brown no more, but most every weekend he could see Josephine coming and going to work right past his window. He'd never seen a big woman move so smooth, like she floated by his window and he wanted to know more about her. But he tried to put her out his mind. She was so dry, hateful almost, and he came here for a job not no woman.

All the women round town, single and married, was a buzzing bout this new man from Alabama that done moved to Stanford. All kind of women got to strutting back and forth down the street right up in Ashe's window but he didn't pay them much mind. Josephine didn't pay them much mind either. She was either too tired from working over time at The Brown or just too tired period to put another man in her mind.

The next time Ashe laid eyes on Josephine it was at church. Josephine came in with her children, each of them in a straight line following behind their mama like they had proper home training. They were all a sight to see.

Josephine settled herself and her young-uns in the pew. She looked straight ahead toward the pulpit when Jewell and Maylene walked in. It wasn't til the deacon called on visitors did Josephine really hear Ashe's voice for the first time. She was rested and peaceful in church with her ears wide open. Ashe stood up in the back of the church when visitors was called on and all the women in the church turned to look. Ashe's voice moved cross the church like a note in a jazz song.

"Just glad to be a member of this community and to be in the house of the Lord with you all here today. Thank you for having me." That's all he said but a feeling went out over the women in the crowd like ain't nobody ever seen. Josephine heard him loud and clear.

After church every woman alive was gathered round Ashe Yerby offering to bring him casseroles, cakes and cobblers, offering to help him with whatever he needed. And I'm sure each of them was serious as cancer bout what they was saying.

Ashe searched the crowd for Josephine but looked out and saw her and her children walking hand-in-hand away from him. "Miss Josephine," he hollered breaking away from the mob of church women. "Miss Josephine, wait." His voice, cool as water, bounced off Josephine's ears like springtime. She turned round and saw the whole women's congregation behind Ashe with their hands on their hips. "I just wanted to compliment you on the sight that you and your children are. They are the most well-behaved children, to be so little, I think I've ever seen and you are quite a vision, too."

"Thank you, Mr Yerby," Josephine said and kept on stepping, relishing the fact that he remembered her name. Ashe headed in the other direction, relishing the same feeling.

Ashe started hanging out at The Brown regular when Josephine was working. He'd sit at the counter and talk to her for hours between customers. He'd talk til his throat was dry then she'd bring him some ice tea or lemonade over and they'd talk some more. Jewell and George Elvis both noticed but couldn't neither one of them say a word. All them women in need of a man took notice too.

Wasn't too long til Ashe was picking up Josephine and the kids for long drives out in the country and taking her to work or walking her to work, depending on the weather. Two or three months went by fore Josephine really invited Ashe to her house. He came over for dinner, ate with her and the kids, helped her put them all down for bed and went home.

One night, fore things got too far down the road, Josephine sat Ashe down and told him bout her whole life. Told him bout her mama and daddy . . . all her baby's daddies, including Jewell Barker . . . Jewell's visits to see Steve Edward . . . George Elvis . . . and everything else there was to tell.

She expected to see his backside headed out the door after that long story but he pulled her close to him. Josephine opened her mouth for a kiss cause she knew he wanted to get some of her after hearing bout what everybody else done got but he just pulled her close and held her tight. "Damn, woman you been dragged down the river and back again, ain't you? Well, long as I'm living you won't go that way no more," was all he said. Josephine let loose of bout ten years of tears on Ashe that night. He held her and wiped her face and whispered cool words in her ear like a mama comforting a sick child. When she fell off to sleep, he stretched her out on the couch and covered her up. When

Josephine woke up with panic in her eyes, Ashe had already got the kids dressed, gave them some breakfast and had her waitressing uniform pressed and ready.

On Monday nights, Ashe greeted Jewell Barker at the door, invited him in and told him that Steve Edward was waiting on him in the kitchen. Jewell was in some kinda shock but he visited with his son and left without a word to Josephine except, hello.

Guess six months had passed before Ashe really took Josephine in his arms. But when he did, they both was more than ready. He kissed her in tiny, soft kisses and long hard kisses, stopping to ask if she liked this or that. She did the same for him. They explored each other, stopping to check if each other was all right. He made love to Josephine like a man in love and that was something she had never had. They laid in a heap as high as love would stack up and when morning creeped in, Ashe had nowhere and nobody to run off to and they made love all over again before the kids got up.

Ashe and Josephine began to go everywhere together. They went to church, the grocery store and to each other's work, always with his hand at her waist. They sat in church and she patted him lovingly on the knee or held his hand. Every woman in all of Stanford went wild. It just didn't make no sense to them at all. So they would corner Ashe when he was by hisself and try to tell him some of Josephine's business, what little they knew. But he always knew bout what they was telling him and more so he'd shut them up quick.

Come the next spring, Ashe and Josephine got married at the church. The whole town turned out for the wedding just to see if it was true, some fine, hard-working man all out in the open with Josephine Childs and marrying her to boot.

Josephine was a vision sure nuff with her hair all down round her shoulders, joy pouring out her face and a great, long lavender dress touching the floor. She had both Jewell Barker and George Elvis wanting to reach out to her, cause they was remembering old times, but they couldn't. And Ashe all dressed in white, a smile cross his face a mile long, his voice booming out vows to love Josephine forever. All three of her kids stood up with her, a sight to see. And the whole town bout tipped over with everybody traveling to the edge, bending their ears to the door.

Mules

"Come on, you chicken?" Lottie said. "It ain't gonna hurt you. It's just gonna make you into a real woman. It's what women do. Your mama's done it. My mama, Aunt Fannie, they all done it before. All he gonna do is like this." She reached out and pinched both my titties real hard and then grabbed between my legs and smiled. "See that's all you got to do. Just stand there while he does it. You don't have to smile or nothing and he'll give us both a dollar. Course if you let him feel you up under your clothes he'll go as high as three but I ain't thinking you quite ready for that."

"No, not quite," I says back, looking at her like Mama does Daddy when she ain't believing he had the nerve to say what he says. "I just don't think it's right to be lettin nobody touch your privates. Lessen it's your mama washing you. And we both too old for that. It just ain't right. A fully grown man too. Girl you done fell plumb out your tree. That don't make you no woman. If it does I'll just stay right like I am."

"Well, I might be crazy all right," Lottie says. "But you tell me where else you gonna get five dollars round here without cleaning up some white folks' house from sun up to sun down or takin in a bushel barrel of washing or doin some kind of other white folks' work."

"How you hide all that money from Aunt Sophie?"

"Well, I hide my money up under a board this side of the corn crib in the barn. There's this one loose board and I got a cigar box up under it. Got close to fifteen dollars saved up now. Course, all that didn't come from old man Wesley. Most of it I just saved up myself from takin in washin, gatherin black walnuts, diggin for ginseng roots, blackberries . . ."

I don't believe a word the girl is saying. I can tell by the way her forehead's wrinkling right between her eyes that she's lying. I been knowing Lottie all my life—all our lives. I suspect that every penny in that cigar box done come from dirty carryings-on with old man Wesley and my stomach commences to turn flip-flops at the thought.

I could just picture Lottie all skinny and straight up like a tree standing half naked in a cornfield or a field somewheres letting some old chapped-face geezer touch her in a nasty way.

And I had done heard Mama and Aunt Fannie talking

in the kitchen bout what a pretty girl Lottie would grow up to be if her being high yellah and having good hair didn't ruin her.

And it didn't seem like being high yellah and having good hair had ruint her as far as I could tell, but I was beginning to wonder about this meeting in the cornfield. I knew deep down that being a woman just couldn't have nothing to do with letting some old man feel up under your skirt.

Grandmama says, "Pretty is what you make it", and color—be it yellow, brown or blue-black—ain't never carried black folks for long. I guessed it was up to me to bring her back to her senses.

"Lottie," I said, before I had thought on my words too long, "you gonna ruin your high-yellah self." I wasn't even sure if I was saying the right words, but I had heard Grandma Hazel giving all the women we knew advice and it sounded like something she might say. "You gonna be ruint and everybody's gonna call you an old cat-eyed yellah ruint woman."

Lottie looked at me like Grandma Hazel had just got on her, which she had, through me some kind of way, and tears edged out the sides of her eyes but she wiped them dry with the back of her hand and cut into me quick. "Well, I'll just be ruint then," she said, turning red in the face, coming to herself and realizing that I was just Ora Lee and not Grandma Hazel at all. "And I'll be a ruint, cat-eyed, high-yellah something with more money in her pocket than you've ever seen. I'll be a ruint, rich, high-yellah something that's for sure—with fancy clothes, real silk stockings, and diamond earrings, and high-heeled shoes," Lottie said and stomped across the field. "And don't you come around asking me for a darn thing," she hollered over her shoulder.

I realized that I wasn't nowhere near being Grandma Hazel when I couldn't think of anything else to say. I ran after Lottie, chasing her through the branch and to the edge of the cornfield.

"Look, see Lottie," I said sucking in breath when I caught up to her. "That old shit ain't even here. Let's go on back to the house and find something else to do." I slumped over and held my knees, trying to catch my breath.

"Girl, you silly," Lottie laughed, "ain't no man gonna want your silly tail anyway." I picked up a dirt clod and took aim at Lottie's head just as she was rearing it back to laugh some more. The clod busted, making scattering noises like hard rain. Just beyond where the dirt clod splattered into a hundred pieces was old man Wesley, peeking through some cornstalks just grinning.

He peered his red face out from the corn, looking all queer. Black was showing where white teeth must have been at one time or another. A spewing fountain of tar came in our direction as he spit tobacco juice through his use-to-be teeth. He stood cocklegged for a minute just looking at us and rubbing his hands up and down the front of his work jacket. I dropped my head to where all I could see was the hem and pocket of his jacket, his big black boots and the faded knees of his britches.

Lottie walked over to him. I watched, like it was a

picture show, as old man Wesley lifted up Lottie's blouse and rubbed his tobacco-stained hands where her breasts would be if she really had any. Lottie just stood stiff and looked like she was holding her breath.

But she didn't say nothing and I didn't say nothing and old man Wesley didn't say nothing. He didn't even look her dead in the face. He just kept on looking down where he was doing his business. At times, I couldn't even tell if Lottie was even breathing at all, but since she didn't fall dead, I just guessed she had to be sneaking breath somewhere. Old man Wesley lifted up her skirt, ran his hand down in her white cotton panties and moved his hand on her privates. He made sounds through his lips that burnt clean through me like a hot poker in red cinders. Seemed like I couldn't bring myself to look away but at the same time I was wishing I could. Wishing I could run with feet that refused to move. And old man Wesley just kept on looking at where his hands were touching. Grandma Hazel always says that a person who won't look you right in the eye got too many secrets and I suspected this was probably one of the biggest secrets one old white man could have.

After he got through rubbing on Lottie, he sucked through his lips some more, breathed out one big time and bowed his head down so low that I thought he was gonna say a blessing over Lottie, then he stopped, stepped back from Lottie and turned toward me.

"Comere gal," he said real low-like while he was stepping closer. "You needing a few dollars in your pocket, too?" He pulled money from his shirt pocket and began rolling off dollar bills as he stepped closer. "No," I tried to scream but it came out as a whisper, surprising even me, but I meant it none the less. Lottie had put her clothes back straight. She turned her back and stood swaying—hugging herself about the arms and rocking. Old man Wesley put his hands on the front of my blouse, grinning like he knew all this was new to me. My scream found itself and I hollered like I had never hollered before. "No! I don't want your damned old money and don't you lay one finger on me!" I kicked him in the shin as hard as I could.

The wad of money he had been holding fell on the ground. Lottie turned around during the commotion, scooped up the money, grabbed my hand and we took off running—jumping branches, taking shortcuts til we reached the barn. We collapsed on some bales of hay and laughed nervous giggles til we cried and then cried til we laughed.

Lottie showed me her cigar box and put twenty more dollars in it. She passed me ten. On Saturday I went to town with Grandma Hazel, Mama and Daddy. I looked for something to buy in the Ten Cents Store but just couldn't bring myself to buy nothing. I felt just like I did that time when I had slipped a piece of cinnamon candy in my coat pocket at Sherman's Store. I couldn't enjoy the candy at all and had ended up feeding it to Miss Catherine's one-eyed hound.

After I decided I couldn't buy nothing with the money, I ran to the back of the store to catch up to Daddy, who was counting loose number-three nails into a brown paper bag in the hardware corner. As I watched him counting the nails, old man Wesley limped up the aisle toward us. He started to pass on by but Daddy stopped counting and turned toward him.

"Howdy do, Wesley? What the heck happened to you?" I moved closer to Daddy's side, slipped my hand into the hammer slot on his overalls and held on tight.

"Oh, it was the damndest thing," old man Wesley said, keeping his eyes toward the floor as he passed us. "Got kicked by a wild mule, bout killed me."

"Mules is stubborn," Daddy said, laughing. "Guess that'll be a lesson to you."

The next day after church Miss Catherine spent all afternoon trying to figure out who gave that ten dollar donation to the building fund and didn't fill out no pledge card.

Ritual

I sit here again with this belly ache. I watch my own brown hand rubbing this tender spot as if it is a hand belonging to a stranger. My fingers massage this belly. Soft, pliable. Sometimes I push in gently trying to feel the source of this worry.

Soon, I will lie on my back in the comfort of a Lone Star quilt stitched by my mother. Tonight, I will play Billie Holiday, again. Lift my nightgown and skim this stomach. Kneading my own flesh. Stopping to plunk here and there to hear its hollow sounds. When my closed eyes bring sleep, I will feel the flutter of butterflies beneath my belly.

James will call me to bed soon. I can hear him rustling the covers. We must wait to see if our prayers are answered. He does not understand that I do not want this place touched now. That this basin is atop some sacred ground. This is a woman's ritual. I will kiss his forehead and his lips. But that is all I am willing to do now. The rest will have to appear in some dream he will be snoring toward before I reach the bed.

Tess and Lou Lou are in my dreams. We three cinnamon-dipped girls, wading in the creek til our feet are wrinkled. We lie out on a blanket up under the sun's brightest eye. See our world through the shapes of clouds. Watch the blue of the Indian Creek sky. We hope that motherhood will swoop down on the backs of blue jays. That horizon-kissed feathers will float babies into the fleshy mounds of our nine-year old bellies. Eyes close. We pray that spiraling pine needles will land between our legs and make us bleed.

I was twelve when the hurting blood came. Found the color of burnt sugar between my legs. Mama said, "It's the beginning of a woman's glorious suffering, child. Just the beginning." Mama wrapped her indigo arms around me. I can still smell her kiss. It is burrowed behind my right cheek.

I sit here near the window, my hands upon my waist. I watch the birth of night up over Patsy Riffe Ridge. I hear the creek's waters from just down the hill. I can feel the moon's tug on the life-strand that ropes from my navel. It is a strange feeling.

Last night I told James that a woman should be able to hear such a powerful thing as procreation if she just gets still. So I listen. Hush and wait. But the body is a defiant vessel. I cannot hear a thing. I imagine a crew of laborers inside this wall. Checking tubes and passageways. Pruning for the next harvest.

When we were married, I wore purple in celebration. Me and James all sunshine and musk in Nana's backyard. Each of us veiled in July's sweat. Mama in her orange-sherbet tea length. Counting the numbers and naming the names of her unborn grandchildren on her fingers one by one. When she reaches five, her voice disappears behind the band. But I see her lips moving around in the music. See her hands move to her hips. ". . . and Douglas Catherine. Now that one will be named for me." I know what she's saying. I've heard all their names so many times. I feel like I know these imaginary children. Like I have always been their mother. Back then I smiled at Mama's fabulous notion.

Now James is out of bed. The wood creaks under his feet. He comes to me. His eyes bright as the stars. His head cocked like a sleepy child. He kneels to the floor. Places his head on my lap, his cheek resting in the dip between my thighs. When he sighs I feel his breath. His arms are lost somewhere around my hips.

"Please come to bed," he says, each word bouncing off the top of my thigh.

"Soon," I say.

He kisses my leg through the thin cotton of my night-gown. For a moment my eyes are closed and I am receptive to his invitation. But this cannot happen tonight. There are forces at work within my body.

"No," I whisper. "Not yet."

James does not fully understand that I want nothing

to interfere with the possibility of this miracle. He looks at me with a begging light in his eye. I cup his face in my hands. Pull him toward my face until our lips touch.

"I love you. You know that?" I say.

"I know," he says.

I embrace my husband. Over his shoulder the sky is a fresh, bright sprinkling of stars. The moon is full, round. I kiss his forehead. Kiss his lips again before he heads to bed alone.

Later I hear James snoring softly. I am pleased at the peace of him and his delicate breathing. I smile then run my hands from belly to thighs in his honor.

Mama says she has never seen any woman quite like me. That in all her born days she has never seen a woman with these strange ways. Never seen a woman so bound and determined. I rub this tender place, trying to quench this ache. Take in Billie Holiday's voice like water. Tonight when my closed eyes bring sleep, I will feel a tiny mouth pull on my breast. Smell my own sweet milk. A caramel face will lie in the crook of my arm. Warm.

The Wonderer

Many a night Javeda would lie on her back and be lulled by katydids and whippoorwills speaking to one another in the pitch of the Casey Creek night. A cool breeze would rustle her nightgown and she would lie still and awake, paying close attention to the quiet of the darkness. The leaves rustling in the air like a woman's skirt tail, the dampness of the night, the chirping of a far-off bird. She'd make hand-puppet shadows on the yellowed wallpaper as the moon shined its fullness into her bedroom window. Sometimes, with her nose pressed against a mason jar full of lightning bugs, Javeda would watch the blue-green florescent off-and-on glow and set to thinking. She would wonder why white folks seemed to have life so easy and why black folks seemed to have so many stumbling blocks.

After all as Granny Tine said, "We was travelin' through the exact same life as them." Sometimes she even wondered what it'd be like if she rose up in the morning a white girl. A white girl like Paula, who lived at the end of the gravel road. All fragile-like with bone straight hair, jet black like Brownie's mane and tail. Like some fragile china doll spending her time sitting somewhere just looking pretty with people, both grown and children, making a fool over her. And that hair she got, all straight and easy on a comb. Javeda wondered how'd Paula feel wedged between the sturdy legs of her Gran Nan or Granny Tine while her locks were being coaxed into behaving. Javeda guessed the flip side of that coin was that maybe, just maybe, Paula would never know the love that comes outta them hour-long combing spells, be it Gran Nan or Mama or Granny Tine who was doing the combing.

That's how Javeda got to the heart of her women folk. Sitting with her hair weaving in and out of somebody's fingers. That's where souls got transferred. That's where knowledge was passed on. She liked that time between sturdy black legs, feeling the love being greased into her scalp. And what kinda patience could a fifteen-minute hair combing learn you anyhow. Javeda guessed if she didn't wake up black as pitch every morning that maybe, just maybe, there wouldn't be no need in digging that deep, all the way down to the soul for strength. She figured that if her skin wasn't blue-black she'd have to learn to laugh from her mouth and not her belly. It wouldn't be necessary anymore to force a giggle through some pain to make the pain go away. Javeda decided that she wasn't even sure if she'd appreciate the beans and turnips on the table if she didn't help pick 'em for herself. And Granny Tine and Gran Nan always said that a girl who won't work don't deserve no good, hardworking man. Javeda thought she might get tired of sitting on cushy chairs all day watching the world pass her by through a looking-glass. Finally decided that every morning God blessed her with she'd wake up black so she'd have to learn to deal with everything that came with it. After her long spell of mind wondering, she'd roll over in her bed, bid the lightning bugs good night and try to be thankful for being black as the sky.

Deviled Eggs

Addie Bea gathered up her Lone Star quilt, her two favorite dolls—Polly and Anne—and a tiny blue pot from a doll tea set. She placed them carefully in the bottom of the white cotton sack she dragged behind her most mornings.

"Addie Bea," her daddy hollered in to her, "you gonna make your mama late to work."

She kissed her teddy bear, Bo, on the nose.

"Sorry Bo, you'll have to go tomorrow," she whispered in his ear.

Emmitt T. and Oline, stood outside the back door waiting for their daughter. Emmitt T. paced back and forth across the short length of the rock steps while he spun the skeleton key, which dangled from a string, around his forefinger. Oline held the screen door open, tapping her foot anxiously on the packed dirt that made a half circle around their back door.

"Lord, here she comes with all that stuff again," Oline said shaking her head. "This child gonna make Miss Lula mad for sure. You know she don't take much a likin to kids anyhow."

"Girl, put all that ole stuff up under the kitchen table and bring your self on out this house," Emmitt T. said. "Now," he said when she hesitated.

Big sad tears rolled down Addie Bea's cheeks as she squeezed into the front seat of the truck beside her parents.

"Mama, I don't want go to Miss Lula's," she tried to explain through wet eyes. "I don't like her, looking like an old haint. Biscuit dough, Elmer's glue looking . . ."

"Well, I don't care if you like her or not," Oline fired back.

". . . like an old haint," Addie Bea mumbled under her breath.

"And don't you go calling your elders names—be they black, white or green," Oline said.

"You going and I don't want to hear no more bout it. And don't bother that woman for nothing today. You best behave yourself. You hear me?"

"Yes ma'am."

Addie Bea continued to cry and wished she could work the farm with Emmitt T. today. And her mama always did say that she was her daddy made over. So why couldn't she go with him.

She pursed her lips to ask, but when she looked up at her mama's face she could see there weren't no use in wasting breath asking.

Addie Bea's summers were most always spent playing in well-kept yards and roaming through other folks' houses while her mama worked for first one then another white family. If they had kids, though, she didn't roam. Sometimes the kids made fun of her clothes or called her names.

Like Red Pete and his brother Re-Pete, of course that wasn't their real names, except the Pete part, but everybody called them that cause they was brothers with the same name. They called her names all the time, like pickaninny and jigaboo, but after Addie Bea beaned their heads with a rock or two, they seemed to get all right. They had even managed to play ball together once they saw how good she could throw.

When the people her mama worked for didn't have kids or it was an old person whose kids were grown up and moved out, Addie Bea would bring her toys and pretend like she, Oline and Emmitt T. lived in the houses. They were always nicer than her own house, with big white columns on the outside and fluffy carpet that feet could get lost down in on the inside.

But Addie Bea did not like Miss Lula. Her face wasn't pretty and her ways weren't either. She was without doubt the ugliest woman that Addie Bea had ever seen. The wrinkles in her face were cut deep like cracks in a dry creek bed. And always in the front of Addie Bea's mind was the day that Miss Lula had called her a "nigra girl" and Oline had just kept on dusting and humming "Amazing Grace" real low. That night she had asked "why", but Oline and Emmitt T., they just looked at each other and told her that still waters run deep.

"I'm gonna go get James today," Emmitt T. said, raising his voice a little above the rattling of the pickup truck. "I'm gonna try to get that field plowed, graded and sowed fore the rain hits. I smell it comin but the moon is right for plantin today."

"Yeah, look like rain'll be here fore long—round bout suppertime," Oline answered, looking out the front truck window toward the sky.

Addie Bea looked up at the sky, too, but she couldn't figure out what her folks were talking about.

"Looks blue to me," she said.

"Looks sometimes deceivin, girl. Things ain't always what they seemin to be. Sometimes folks got to see thangs other ways cept with they eyes," Emmitt T. said and winked and nodded toward Oline.

They followed the path of the gravel road till it ended and Emmitt T. turned the truck onto pavement. White houses peered above green hills and continued to get bigger as they got closer to town. Emmitt T. pulled into the white gravel driveway of Miss Lula's house, got out and came around and opened the passenger door for Addie Bea and Oline.

"See y'all this evenin," he said.

"Bye, Emmitt," Oline said and kissed her husband on the crest of his bald head.

"Bye, Daddy," said Addie Bea in her softest "Daddy's little girl" voice.

Emmitt T. kissed her pouting lips.

"Bye, baby girl," he said.

He shut the door, ran back around to the driver's side, jumped in and sped back toward the farm. "My Daddy ain't never been one to be too long in town," Addie Bea thought to herself. "He's sure nuff in a hurry to get on back to what's his." At least that's what her mama had said from time to time as they stood on mornings like these, watching him speed off into the distance.

Oline's shoe heels clicked against the concrete as she walked up the sidewalk to the entrance of Miss Lula's house. Addie Bea stalled in the driveway as long as she could, kicking white gravel dust on her brown shoes and watching the path of her daddy's truck long after it was clean out of sight.

"Girl, come on here," Oline called. "And stick your lip back in fore I pull it off."

Miss Lula opened the door and poked her head out. Small bits of color, yellow streaks in her white hair and her fading blue eyes, gave her face some life. Other than that she was equally white from the top of her head to her neck, where the pink of her dress began.

"Oh, it's you, Oline," she said opening the door for both of them but ignoring Addie Bea. "I didn't know who this colored woman was on my step."

"Mornin Miss Lula," Oline said letting the foolish comment slip on elsewhere. Addie Bea walked into the screened porch, avoiding Miss Lula's face. She chose being ignored over being patted on the head, which Miss Lula was inclined to do at times.

It always made Addie Bea's insides churn to see her mother running around saying "yes ma'am" and "no ma'am" to white folks that weren't any more grown-up than she was. The inside-out feeling stayed with her all day and resentment settled like sediment in the pit of her belly.

"Oline, I don't need a whole lot done today," Miss Lula said sashaying away, her back to Oline. "If you could just touch up each room, clear out the pantry and freshen up the icebox that'll be fine. And I'm taking company this evenin. I'll cook and get the linen off the line, if you'll just make sure they are washed. You can save your ironing for Wednesday."

"Yes ma'am," Oline said. "I don't see much problem ma'am but it's gonna rain this evenin and . . ."

"Don't be daft girl," Miss Lula laughed, turning to face Oline. "Look, not a cloud in the sky," she said pointing toward the window. "You coloreds with your hoo-doo and what have you—thinkin you can predict the weather." Miss Lula turned her back and laughed real snooty-like all the way into the other room.

Chills ran up and down Addie Bea's spine like she had just sucked the juice out of a lemon.

"Go on out in the backyard," Oline whispered to Addie Bea. "Just play out there for a little while. I'll call you when it's time for lunch. I got a couple of sandwiches wrapped in wax paper down in my pocketbook."

Oline kissed Addie Bea on her top plait and patted her lovingly on the backside as she skipped off to play. "Stay in line, child," Oline whispered as much to herself as to her baby girl.

Addie Bea stood in the middle of the backyard looking around for something she could do without her dolls and her teapot. Between the rose bush and the walnut tree looked perfect for the tea party she had planned, but she'd have to make do without them.

Addie Bea lay on her back in the grass looking up in the clear blue sky. Blades of grass pierced the backs of her legs and pierced through her cotton jumper. She stood up.

"Oline, I don't need a whole lot done today. I'm having a tea party," Addie Bea said to the emptiness of the yard. She put one hand on her hip and jumped to the other side. "Look you ole pasty-face heifer, I ain't gonna work my fingers to the bone fooling with your ole house," her imitation Oline voice fussed back. "Sides, ain't you got the blasted sense to see that it's gonna rain?"

"Well, I'm gonna fire you. I don't like your girl, anyway."

"Well, fine. Then I quit."

Addie Bea stormed across the yard, walking her mother's walk.

She soon lost track of time. As the morning moved on she claimed every corner of the yard for her own.

She played a concert to the trees at the edge of the woods that surrounded the far ends of Miss Lula's yard.

She sang and played her own mouth horn formed by a blade of grass placed between her thumbs.

Down the hill was her school; First Smell Good Baptist Church was over by the fence row; and her fishing hole was the concrete slab over the cistern.

"Addie Bea," Oline yelled out the back door of the porch. "Come on in here and get your sandwich out my pocketbook. I'm still workin and can't take no break right now."

Addie Bea followed her mother into Miss Lula's kitchen.

"The child can eat with me," Miss Lula said appearing from another room wiping her bony wet hands dry on the pleated front of her dress.

"No . . ." Oline starts.

"Why sure I can," Addie Bea interrupts, thinking whatever Miss Lula is cooking has to be better than a half-a-day-old sandwich all squashed in her mama's pocketbook. "I sure am hungry."

Oline's eyes widened to that mama look that all little girls know and her hands flew to her hips. She was about to speak when she was interrupted again. This time by Miss Lula.

"Why Oline, course the child can eat with me. I'm gettin ready to fix myself some lunch right now. I got some leftovers. It's no problem really. Is there a problem?"

Oline didn't finish her sentence and Addie Bea disregarded the look in her mother's eyes even though she knew she'd have to answer later.

Oline began cleaning out the pantry while Miss Lula prepared to cook. Addie Bea put on a real act for Miss Lula.

"Miss Lula, I like your dress," she said. "Mama says you cook real good."

Miss Lula began to warm up the leftovers, while Addie Bea sat on a wooden stool beside the entrance to the back porch and waited. She kicked her shoes one against the other in anticipation. She looked at first one and then the other rose-covered wall and up and down from plastered ceiling to wood floor, dodging her mother's eyes.

Oline had finished the pantry and started in on the icebox before Miss Lula finished.

Addie Bea squirmed on the stool. Her mother's eyes were burning a hole clean through her. She turned her head toward the porch and concentrated on the smells. "Let's see," Addie Bea thought to herself, "roast, new potatoes, greens—no, green beans and a big dessert—apple pie, cobbler maybe."

"Addie Bea, come on and eat," Miss Lula picked up her plate of steak, new potatoes and string beans and sat at the far end of the lemon-oiled wooden table.

She motioned for Addie Bea to sit at the opposite end. Addie Bea walked the long length of the table toward the plate. It was covered with hardboiled eggs from edge to edge. Addie Bea froze in her footsteps.

"Go on gal and sit down, so I can get started on my lunch. Don't you have any manners?" Miss Lula said.

Addie Bea plopped down into the wooden chair so hard she hurt her tailbone.

She eased her teeth into the peeled shiny whiteness. Soft, gooey egg yolk spilled into her mouth.

"Eggs is good for a growin gal," Miss Lula said. "You need some salt?"

Addie Bea shook her head, no.

She edged her mouth open and cupped her hands up to her lips, but her mother raised her head up from inside the icebox and focused her most serious "mama look" right between her daughter's eyes. Addie Bea chewed.

She winced and wiggled back and forth in her chair as she ate, occasionally looking at Miss Lula eating her steak, her wrinkled chin flopping with each bite. After forcing the last half-cooked egg down her throat and drinking two full glasses of water, she rose from her seat. Both women stopped their motions. She quickly sat back down.

"Can I be excused, please?" she pleaded.

Both heads nodded.

Addie Bea returned to Miss Lula's backyard but it was just a yard again now. She lay on her back in the grass and let the blades prick her skin like dull needles. She watched the sky above her spinning and turning from bright blue to hazy white. She watched the sun struggle to shine through the clouds.

She just lay there watching the sky playing tag with the sun until she heard Emmitt T.'s truck pulling onto the gravel. She heard voices coming from the back porch but she didn't move.

"Yes, I got everything done, Miss Lula," Oline was saying, "cept that load of bed clothes I put out on the line this mornin. You sure you don't want me to go round the side and get it? Rain ain't far off."

"There you go with that hoo-doo again. I told you there's no chance of rain today," Miss Lula said.

"Come on Addie Bea," Oline said.

Addie Bea jumped to her feet and glimpsed Miss Lula placing a crisp five-dollar bill in her mother's hand as she ran toward the truck.

"See you Wednesday," Miss Lula said to Oline, acting like Addie Bea was never there.

Just as Oline and Addie Bea settled in the truck and Emmitt T. shifted into reverse, a clap of thunder broke loose and hard rain drops started beating down on the truck.

"Got it plowed just in time, baby," Emmitt T. said smiling at Oline, his shirt still wet with the day's sweat. "Good," Oline said as she kissed his sweaty face and patted her left hand on his right knee. "Good."

"What we gonna have for supper tonight sweet woman? I sure done worked up an appetite today." Emmitt T. said reaching over to squeeze Oline on the portion of her big bronze leg that peeked from beneath her skirt.

"Don't know," Oline said, staring out the window smiling. "But whatever we having, a big mess of deviled eggs sure sounds good to go with it—don't you think so, Addie Bea?" she asked, looking over at her daughter.

Addie Bea held her belly, pressed her forehead against the coolness of the window, prayed for more rain.

Waiting on the Reaper

I'm going nigh on eighty and been waiting on the reaper for sixty-three years now. Been waiting for him to take me away since the day my mama passed on. "Bessie, girl, it's two things you can't rush," she always told me, "life and death." Mama always said babies never come before their time and that those dying know when it's their time to go. So when Mama died, I sat up way into the night waiting for the reaper to come, but he never did.

Of course, I was always wondering how death worked even as a little child. I used to watch a stuck hog writhing on the ground at hog-killing time, wondering what he was thinking. Wondering how it felt when peace covers you up like a quilt. I can still see them hogs' faces, squealing and hollering cause they know it's their time, then finally laying still and going quiet.

Mama went quiet. She'd been sick a long time. Fighting and getting better then getting worse again and starting over. One day she just told me, "Baby, won't be long now, time to give on up in this one and trade this life for the one on the other side." It wasn't two days before she was gone. I was with her, right by her side. Her last few breaths were the deepest, clearest breaths she'd took in since the pneumonia set in. But they was deep, clear breaths. Then she looked up at me and left. And I begged the reaper to take me right then, but he never did.

When my mama went away from here and while I was waiting for my turn with death, Hatley came a courting. He was handsome all right, I guess, if you interested in that sorta thing, courting and all, but I didn't pay him too much mind cause I just wasn't thinking toward them kind of things.

After Mama died I went to live with my Granny Irene, my mama's mama. I set on the porch most days just a thinking about mama and them hogs and the calves I'd seen slaughtered, the chickens, old man Hector up Possum's Branch, everything and everybody that I'd seen dying or dead. Granny Irene would come out and give me breakfast, lunch and dinner right while I was sitting on that porch and then she'd come help me in to bed. She never got after me none though, said everybody had their own way of grieving.

Hatley would come and sit himself down beside me.

Most times for a long time I didn't even hear what he was saying cause I was too busy waiting. Mama died right in the middle of the spring. I never did think too highly of the Lord for that, even though I know it's a sin to think bad of the Lord. Just didn't seem right for all the flowers to be blooming and birds to be chirping and animals hurrying about when my mama was dead to the world. Then one day, Hatley gets right up in my face and grabs me by both shoulders.

"Gal," he says, "I been trying to ask you to marry me for a good month and you ain't said kiss my ass or nothin."

"Well then, kiss my ass," I say back and keep on thinking about how long it's gonna be before I die. But Hatley, I guess, wasn't no giver up. He came by every day, rain or shine, all through the summer, bringing me blackberries and daisies and grapes and watermelons. I'd wait til he left and then look at what he brought me. I began thinking about dying less and less and the silence became just a jig I was pulling on Hatley. I was hearing his words now. I just went on pretending not to.

"I think you're a nice woman," Hatley was a saying. "You're a pretty woman and it ain't like you don't know me. We done both lived here in Summerset all our lives. I've known you since we was kids. Always did think you was pretty, with that long, lean neck of yourn. I never did understand why you was always hangin your pretty head down. I always wanted to catch your eye but you never would hold your head up long enough. Then I heard you moved over here with Miss Irene when your mama died.

133

And, well, I've had my eye on you for years and never got much chance to talk to you and ain't gettin much chance now cause you don't ever say nothin. I mean I know you grievin somethin fierce with your mama passin on and all but I just don't see why you won't give a man a chance. I been comin over here half the spring and all summer long. It's goin on fall and a man can't just keep on runnin after one woman who don't want to give him the time of hour and I ain't gonna come back if you don't talk to me right now on this porch today. I . . ."

"You talk too much."

"Well, you won't talk—what else am I sposed to do?"

"Hatley Purvis, you talk too much, always have. I remember when we was in school with one another you talked more than the teacher."

We both busted out laughing and got it all started.

By the first snowfall me and Hatley was husband and wife. I was a brand new twenty-one. Thought I'd put off dying till after my wedding day. But that night it all came back. Now being a pure girl I didn't know much about husband-and-wife-in-the-bed workings and I don't think Hatley knew much about it either. We fumbled around over each other and Hatley got to wiggling round . . . now I know ladies ain't sposed to talk about these type things but I'm old enough to talk about what I please . . . so he got to wiggling round and couldn't stop and I was squealing and wallowing round in pain cause my insides felt like they was being torn out and I closed my eyes tight and wished for the reaper to come, but he never did.

But you know after that first night Hatley and me both got the hang of husband-and-wife-in-the-bed workings and got to it as much as we could. We lived in a little two-bedroom house that we put a down payment on off his wages at Summerset Saw Mill. He was working down at the mill. So I'd scurry around the house all day and wait for my husband to come home. I'd fix him a big meal, light the fireplace and wait on him. Mama never left my mind, though. Ain't left my mind right today.

I reckon I was happy all right but death thoughts didn't never quite let me alone. Every once in a while when one of the little critters around outside the house would die, I'd stand over it a long while staring at its closed eyes, wondering how it felt. The tomcat Hatley got to kill the mice was walking across the yard one time with a half-live mouse hanging from its mouth. I about had to kill that cat over that mouse but I cupped it in my hands and took it around the back of the house and watched it take in its last breaths and peace cover its little furry face.

135

Most days I didn't do nothing like that, though. Hatley had rubbed some of the pain out my heart and I loved him more and more each day for that. We spent a lot of time together doing different things that couples fool in love do—staring in each other's eyes for hours, cooing and purring and laying still all hugged up.

We never even discussed children. Don't know why, don't ask me. It just never came up til the very day I ended up in a family way. When I told Hatley, his face lit up bright. He picked me up and swung me around. And stood up and sit down and stood up and sit down over and over like a raving fool til I made him sit on down.

"We, you and me, us together, we, you mean the two of us, gonna have a baby?" he stuttered out.

"Well, I don't see no other folks in this room that's gonna have a baby, do you?"

We both laughed and wrapped each other up tight. Guess I was around twenty-three when I got in a family way that first time. I grew great big and my body felt unfamiliar. My belly grew tight and miserable. I almost prayed for relief but didn't follow through for Hatley and the baby's sake and for my own.

It was on the anniversary of Mama's death when pains commenced to coming, shooting through me like a butcher knife. Hatley took me in town to the hospital. I laid out across that table with my legs spread-eagle in them holsters for hours and hours. Hatley stood by my side, his temple creased with fear and concern for me and our young one. I writhed around in pain for eighteen hours, with the image of a stuck pig's blood pouring out on the ground at hog-killing time playing in my mind. I could see the pig squealing and writhing in the dirt but there was no sound and then no moving when he went away from this earth. I screamed as loud as I could, for as long as I could when I pushed our son, Hatley Jr out into the world.

"He's not breathing," a doctor said. People dressed in white surrounded our little boy ordering first this one then that one in the white coats to do this or that.

"Make 'em move, Hatley," I said looking up at my

husband. "Make 'em move, I can't see his face. I can't see his face!" Hatley held me back, so I wouldn't jump down off that table. Our boy was dead. The nurses and doctors cleaned him up real good. Said they didn't know what had happened. Said things just happen sometime. Hatley held Junior's little body in his arms and cried into his little chest. I kept waiting on his chest to start rising and falling but it didn't not even once. He was perfect though. A perfect round head with a head of curly, sandy hair. Perfect chubby little brown hands and feet. I closed my eyes and held my son tight. He smelled like a newborn baby, fresh and sweet. I sucked his smell deep in my head. Sucked it deep and tried to make it stay. But it was gone each time I breathed out. I rocked my baby and cried. I could feel Hatley's comforting hands pressed loving-like deep into my shoulders. I knew the reaper was in the room. I whispered for him to please take me. To please take me even out of the comfort of Hatley's hands.

After our firstborn baby died I'd sit outside til Hatley came home watching for any of God's creatures that I could see on the brink of death but I couldn't find none. But soon I had people to watch dying again. Granny Irene passed over five years to the day that Junior was brought into the world dead. She got down real sick before though and I watched over her. "Yeah, ole Irene's done wore down and wore out," she says to me one morning. "Done seen all I want to see and done all I want to do over here on this side and I'm looking forward to meeting my maker and seeing yo mama and yo grandpa and all my other young-uns again. And my mama and Cousin Louvene and . . ."

"Granny Irene," I say trying to get her off death's road, "you gone be all right. Maybe when you get to feeling a little better you can come on and move in with me and Hatley. You sure wouldn't be no trouble and sometimes I get lonesome out there by myself just waiting on him to come home."

"Lord child, no," she says just as big as she wants, "what's an old woman like me doing intrudin on young folks lives. I done already lived mine. Time fo you and yours to live yourn. No, I'm lookin forward to this. I'm ready now. Ain't got too much time. Gonna see Lonnie and my little girlfriend that drowned in a well when I was ten . . ."

And Granny Irene named all the kinfolks and friends that done passed on before the morning ended. Kept on bragging bout how she gone see them all soon, sooner, she say, than everybody thought she was. And sure nuff three or four days, I can't remember now, but she died. Granny Irene's face still grins at me when I close my eyes at night. All wrinkled sweet and smiling all broad, like she had just entered heaven's gate. I don't remember her being that happy in life. And I got down on my knees right beside her bed that evening and prayed and begged old reaper to take me on, but he never did.

When Granny Irene went to glory, I commenced to sitting on the porch waiting again. Hatley seemed to know that it wasn't him I was waiting on. I loved him so, still, but my passion for the other side was strong. I believe it was a Sunday, yeah, I'm pretty sure it was, that day when Hatley went to check on something at the mill. I put on my best dress, brushed my hair down and took every aspirin in the house. I laid down in the bed and waited. Kept calling and calling on that angel of death, praying like nobody's business, trying to get him there, but he never did come. Never did.

Hatley came home to me puking out my guts out the back door. He kind of changed a bit when he found out about me. I never let on, told him I was catching the flu but I know he knew. Seems like he took it personal, though, moped round like a boy lost. But he came around. I tried to be happy for Hatley. We held one another tight like we used to. Course I thought I was way too old by then to be getting in a family way, but it happened. It sure did. Course I was scared, we both was considering what happened to Junior, but everything seemed to go all right as far as I knowed about such things.

Hatley was so happy he commenced to bringing me presents again. It was summer and he brought me grapes and apples and nectarines til I was tight as a tick. It was March when my water broke. I see a clear picture of it all like it was happening right now. I was out in the yard. March winds was picking up. Halfway winter, halfway spring. Blowing cold, then blowing warm. I was sitting out on a blanket in the yard. It was the first warm day and Hatley and me was having us a picnic. We always did silly in-love stuff that way, cause we was indeed in love. Bless his heart, he didn't know what to do next. Pulling me up, dragging me toward the car like a forty-pound sack of potatoes. I didn't know his strength til that day cause I'm a pretty big woman.

In the car we was both quiet. Guess we was both thinking bout Junior but neither one of us said exactly what was on our minds. Pains kept coming over me strong and in a hurry. These pains was worse than the ones I'd had with Junior but I didn't let on. Didn't scream for mercy, not once.

Me and Hatley had us the prettiest little girl you ever did see way up about two or three o'clock in the morning. She was full of life, squalling her little brown head off. Some ole time folks say black babies always light skinned when they born and then they color turns but she came in this world with the color she kept. We named her Lena after some of Hatley's kinfolks, and he was the proudest papa I'd ever seen on this entire earth. That man was crazy about that baby. He would change her diapers and mash up her taters once she got old enough to eat solids. Yeah, I know plenty men do that these days but way back then wasn't no men that I knew of eager to take care of no pissy tailed young-uns. Lena was a handful as a little young-un, pulling out pots and pans, covering herself in flour and cornmeal. Every once in a while I'd get a glimpse out the corner of my eye of something or the other that done fell prey but didn't have much time to focus on dying, since Lena was so full of life and all. Mama and Granny Irene appeared to me in dreams nodding their heads, yes, and looking proud at what a fine mama I was. I didn't see them so much on their death beds anymore but had flashes, visions, of the fine times we'd all had on this side.

I was an ole woman to be having a young-un running and jumping about all the time, but I loved my Lena with all the might I had. Did everything a young mama could do. We played ring around the roses in the pastures, swam in the creek, sung songs and played dress-ups. But time took hold quick. She was in school and my days was back lonely. Nothing to fill me up but old thoughts while her and Hatley was out the house. I went back to watching little creatures round the yard dying.

It was right on the edge of winter round suppertime. Lena was doing her school work at the kitchen table and I was peeling taters at the sink. I kept peeking out the window cause Hatley was true as any clock. I pressed two red streaks down the front of my thighs rubbing my hands on my apron for over an hour worrying. Finally I heard a car pull up the road and heard a door open and shut. Mrs Stevens, Hatley's boss man's wife, was standing on my porch when I got to the door.

"Mrs Purvis," she says to me her face white as talc powder, "there's been an accident. Hatley, well, Hatley has been in an accident and I've come to take you to the hospital to see him."

"He all right?" I say thinking I'm talking normal but my voice speaks out real low-like.

"Mama, what done happened to Daddy?"

"Girl, get your coat on," I say clearin my throat hard,

tryin to get my right voice back. "Go on now, it's cold out."

My head was hurting like it was caught in a vice and I felt like I was down in a hole. Barely hearing. Barely seeing. Everything seemed far-off like. Like I wasn't really right in that spot in my own house. I still remember it all fresh.

I don't remember us getting in the white woman's car but I remember riding down the road smelling her perfume and feeling the cold of the leather clean through my skirt and asking over and over again what happened to my man.

"I'm not sure," she says for the third or fourth time. "Mr Stevens instructed me to stay back. Not to look at what was going on but to go get you and your daughter and take you all to the hospital so you can be with Hatley."

I'd never heard of a woman calling her own husband mister, and I tried to put my mind toward that not toward Hatley.

"Mama, Daddy's gone die, ain't he?" Lena commenced to screaming in the back seat. "Oh Lord, Mama, he gone die."

"Hush, child," I say to my Lena. "We gone see to him in a minute. Just soon as we get up the road here to the hospital."

"Honey, I don't think your daddy's gonna die. Mr Stevens didn't say nothing like that. I mean, I'm sure he's goin to be just fine. Your daddy sure is a good worker. My husband brags on him all the time. He says if he had ten more like Hatley . . ."

Mrs Stevens' words went to a hum, blended on with

the hum of the car and I reached back cross the seat and held Lena's cold trembling hand, rubbing up and down and round her knuckles til we got to the hospital. I looked round for the reaper and hoped he'd choose me right then, but he never did.

Me and Lena ran off from Mrs Stevens, jumped out the car like two women on a mission. I think we said, "thank you", but I can't remember. We held hands walking down the big long hallway. I didn't like hospitals and hoped I didn't die in one. As soon as we saw some people in white coats milling about we started asking bout Hatley.

Every coat we ran into pointed a finger showing us the way. Finally, a doctor came around the corner outa nowhere saying he wanted to talk to me fore he let us see Hatley. He tried to get me to let him send Lena out the room but I wouldn't let him.

"Well, Mrs Purvis," he starts off, pausing after every word, "your husband has received multiple amputations." Mama introduced me to a man once that had both his legs amputated. That's what I was seeing in my mind's eye, that poor man in a wheelchair with no legs. I was still holding on to Lena's hand and squeezed down hard. "His right arm was severed above the elbow so we had to remove it at the shoulder and his right leg has been amputated at the thigh."

He went on talking bout how Hatley fell into some kind of cutting machine over at the saw mill and the thing had chewed on his arms and legs before they got it turned off and got him out. He said it was a miracle that he didn't lose his other leg and that Hatley was in what they call shock. Lena cried her heart dry. I held her close. "Just be glad he ain't dead, chile," I say trying to be of some comfort to my young-un. "Just be glad he ain't gone on way from here."

We both eased our heads round the corner of room 329. Yep, I still remember that too. Guess cause we spent so much time there way back then. I think we was both scared of what kind of mutilated version of Hatley we was gone see. Hatley didn't know we was in the room at first. He just stared out wall-eyed. His head turned toward us when he heard Lena say, "Hi, Daddy," but he didn't talk.

A big tear welled up and flowed out of his right eye. I still don't know to this day what that tear was representing. I don't know if he was hurting so bad or if he was so glad to be alive to see Lena and hear her voice.

She leaned over to her daddy and kissed him on his forehead. I kissed him on his cheek. He was laid out in the bed so nice, the covers pulled up round his neck but I could see the flatness in the bedclothes where his arm and leg use to be. We didn't talk, none of us, in that room for seven straight days. Seems like me and Lena did all our talking at home and down the hallway to the hospital before we reached 329. We'd look at one another, kiss, cry and look, kiss and cry some more but nobody said a word.

It was Hatley himself that broke the silence on that seventh day. "Bessie," he says to me, his voice real hoarse, "I ain't never gone be no use to y'all or nobody else. Man's like a mule—if you lame, ain't much choice but to be put down."

"Aw hush man," I says back to him, "there's more to a man than bein a mule plow. You know we can't get along without you."

Me and Lena came to see him almost every day, catching a ride in with first one neighbor and then the other. That's one thing I can say bout the folks here in Summerset is that don't nobody do without if somebody can help 'em.

Hatley was in the hospital a good three months. I didn't have too much time for thinking bout the reaper spirit's making a journey towards me, but it did cross my thoughts a time or two in them times. Hatley came home right in the dead of winter. A fresh coat of snow laid out cross the ground and it was way late up in the evening. The sun was setting, I believe. Yeah, I remember the sun just ready to go down that day. I scurried round fixing up our bedroom for him and putting down salt and ashes all cross the porch and down the sidewalk to get rid of the ice and snow.

The Stevenses drove him home from the hospital. We was riding home in the Stevenses' car. I don't know why I never learned to drive. Here we had a good car in running condition and here I was having to get all kinds of folks to do stuff for me. But Hatley got in an awful way, when on the way home the Stevenses' car wheels got to spinning on the ice in the road. Mrs Stevens got behind the wheel and me, Mr Stevens and Lena got out to try and push the car on off the spot. Hatley got to cussing and fussing cause he wasn't able to get out and help. Got to carrying on so bad that I had to go back to the car in the middle of it all and try to get him settled. Hurt his pride so bad to see his young-un and his wife doing what he called man's work. We finally got off the slick spot and moved on down the road. Hatley looked out the window watching into the night, his stare cold as the wind itself.

It was a long freezing winter, it sure was, specially on the inside of the house. Hatley wouldn't hardly move out the bed and wouldn't hardly say nothing to me, Lena neither. I didn't bother him too much, though. I figured it was his way of grieving for the limbs he lost.

When spring rolled round, Hatley was willing to be brought out on the porch in a wheelchair. Doctor said he could do fine with a crutch once he learned how to hold his balance but Hatley didn't want no parts of no crutch. He'd sit out on the porch just staring out into the day or night. I tried to make him happy cause he had been a good man, a good father and I loved him so. Took all his two-armed shirts and two-legged britches and fixed them so they wouldn't flop in the wind where the missing part shoulda been. But I had to go out and buy some new shirts cause Hatley wouldn't have no parts of 'em. Hatley sat out on the porch from the time Lena left til she got home from school as long as it wasn't raining. I served him breakfast and lunch right out on that old porch unless it rained. If the rain came he'd holler for me to take him in to the bed cause his body ached him so. On a rainy day Hatley even had pain where his leg and arm were no more.

Bout the time that every Summerset flower was blooming and the days had grown long and hot that year, me and Lena went to work. Hatley's sick check had run out and we had ate a big hole through the savings we had. Lena and me both started working for the Stevenses. Course it felt kinda funny cause Hatley had worked for them so long but we needed the money and went right over when they asked us. Lena mostly tended to their new baby while I tended to the house. Sometimes I wondered where ole reaper was at, specially when sweat was pouring off my head and when I worried so hard bout how Hatley was doing on his own.

Seems like I was missing my dying prayers but it wasn't fore long that my life was moving right back in that direction. Doing housework in a house sides your own is bout the most burdensome work I know. Same goes for raisin some other folks' children. Lena knew all bout that. So when me and Lena headed toward the house, we was more than ready. I'd look at my baby from time to time as we'd head towards home. Seem like she just shot up grown overnight and I told her so. Guess she was round bout a middle teenager then. Yeah, she woulda been round bout fifteen or sixteen. We was walking down the road, head to head almost. I say almost cause she was taller than me by then. That girl coulda ate soup beans off my head if she wanted to. Anyway we walking down the road toward home on this particular day and the first thing we notice is that Hatley ain't sitting on the porch. Every day we'd get Hatley ready before we headed out. Lena would get him a jug of ice water, I'd fix him lunch and put it right in his reach so he'd have it. Then I'd sneak him a slop jar so he could handle hisself while I was gone. He never did want Lena to see him with the jar so I'd send her on out the door and down the way for something and hand it to him as I was stepping off the porch. But Hatley wasn't nowhere on that porch when we got home that day. He was gone, wheelchair and all.

I felt a strangeness in the air so I made Lena stay back. I swung open the door and peeped in the house. Everything was quiet, nothing. I heard the radio playing from me and Hatley's bedroom so I walked slow steps in that direction. Can't remember what was playing though. Don't know why I can't remember what was playing. I walked in that room and all the July heat swept out the room. A bone chill grabbed hold. Hatley laid cross the bed, a hole seeping black crimson in the middle of his chest, leaking bright red through one of his good shirts. A gun . . . don't know where that man got a gun from . . . never knew he had a gun . . . but there he was, holding it in his hand. His leg still part way in the wheelchair like he barely made it onto the bed. I see it plain, still. See it plain as day. And his face so peaceful . . . looked right warm. Anyway Hatley, damn him, took hisself out this world sometime while we was working. I never did let Lena come in the house cause it would have been plain in her mind too. A thought she coulda never got out her head. Just like me. So we buried Hatley, bless his heart, and kept on working for the Stevenses a long while, paid off the house, had a few things. And Lena stayed right here by her mama long as she could. We both took Hatley going way from here hard. Everybody has they own way of grieving you know. Wasn't no other way to take it but hard, though. He was the only husband I knew and the only daddy she knew and we grieved a long while. I'm still grieving over that man.

Guess I thought about death and asked for the reaper so much that he kept coming, but he just wasn't coming for me. He just came to take folks way from me for some reason. Like I said to start with I'm nigh on eighty and I don't know how much one woman sposed to stand. My little Lena passed on last year. Doctor said she had what they call cancer. Here she was taking care of me all these years after her daddy died and I had to end up taking care of her. 'Magine that I done took care of the one that brought me in this world and the one that I brought in the world. She reminded me of Mama on her death bed. My girl was in such, such pain, though. She fought hard, then gave up, and fought hard, then gave up for good. By the end I was glad that mercy came. Yeah, I feel bad to this day that I wasn't awake to see her move on. I was sleeping in a chair side her bed and woke up and she was gone. Guess I'm too old.

Sometimes I sneak out yonder on the porch way up in the night right when the dew hits, hoping at my age I'll catch the pneumonia or some kind of something. Every night I dream of Mama, Hatley, Granny Irene, Lena and Junior. Then I smell blood clear and see stuck pigs writhing in the dirt. I see it clear like it was happening right now.

Need

I watch Joan moving quick across the parking lot, her head down, her walk the gait of a pained woman. I can't help but sum her up, trying to figure out all the whys.

She is thin and still somewhat shapely. Her long, straightened hair is pulled back in a ponytail and she wears a hat made out of that artificial African cloth, the kind that you see everywhere these days, even in the dollar store. She is strolling her best self into Gloria's Café with something to prove, her heels just a clicking on the sidewalk in a sing-songy rhythm, but worry shows in her drooping shoulders.

She walks in smelling like musk and my head is swimming in a whole sea of regrets. This is *my* favorite restaurant and I don't want it tainted by this meeting. What if we can't make it through this little get-together?

She is dark, her face heavy with makeup, but it is the same long face, the same jawbone, an older version of the little girl I saw smiling at me from a picture on Evin's coffee table, just an older version.

"Hello, I'm glad you made it," I say and extend my hand out to her, "I'm . . ."

"I know who you are and I am *Mrs* Miller." She ignores my handshaking attempt and so I let my hand drop slow and deliberate to my side.

"Glad you came," I say again trying to keep calm, thinking that somehow it would rub off on her.

I take a long sigh deep inside myself and follow the hostess to a booth next to the window. The hostess is young, that fresh spry young that shows in the wide left-to-right swing of her hips. I smile, remembering those days when my youth was upon me and I was carried along with it by the swing of my hips like her. "Sass-a-frass," Mama would say and I would switch on.

She shows us a window seat. The sun shines through the window, spreading light out across the tablecloth in bright white slivers. It would be a perfect spot for old friends and maybe that's what she thinks we are. Usually, I would love to sit there, eat good food, have good conversation and enjoy the warm of sunlight through a window on my face, but not for this. The glaring sun feels like a spotlight shining on this situation for all the world to see.

"Can we sit back there?" I point to a booth in the shadows, a far-off corner of the place.

"Sure," the hip-swinging girl says, snatching up the

menus, and makes her way in the opposite direction. I follow and can feel Joan's eyes boring holes into my head. My mama's words come: "If looks could kill . . ."

"Richard's your server," that girl says and throws the menus on the table.

"Lord have mercy," I say, "guess she's having a bad day."

Joan just sits and stares down at her water glass, rubbing her finger nervously around the rim.

I bathe myself all up in the walls. I have never noticed the detail of the vines and tree limbs painted all the way across the café's wall. I follow a vine up the corner and there is a thin crack. And just between the vine and that crack is a tiny, purple frog with yellow and orange spots. And just above that is a bright yellow bird, its mouth red and opened wide.

"So, how long have you been fucking my husband?"

It comes out like in a child's whisper somewhere beneath the bowed head. Joan still focused down on the rim of her water glass, drawing circles around and around the edge like a mad woman. All I can see is the orange, yellow and green patterns of the hat on her head. I look from the yellow bird poised to scream to the top of Joan's head. Back and forth, dizzy with the question and the twirling colors. We are two miserable mirror images, us women, mothers, strong black women, reduced to shambles and gone stark raving mad over a situation with a man.

"How long?"

Joan's voice rises to just above normal and our eyes

lock just long enough but not too long. Then I go back to the bird and she back to the glass's rim. I open my mouth the smallest bit to speak. I can feel my mouth working but words aren't coming out.

"Hello Miss Florine, it's good to see you. You looking good as ever."

Richard's deep voice and warm smile is like the sun I am missing from my spot at the window. I stand up and give him a solid hug. Joan fidgets with her silverware and napkin. On the surface I wish I had picked a more neutral spot for this meeting but down deep I am pleased to be smack dab in familiar at Gloria's Café. I am glad to see Richard's handsome, friendly face. I notice a tiny scar just above his eyebrow and the way the ends of his baby dreads curl just the littlest bit. I have never really focused on him hard like this before. This man knows just about all my business, but he doesn't know about my situation with Joan.

I'm in Gloria's Café every week. I love the way it sits right on the corner of Jefferson and Second. Just in the right spot, right down the middle between two worlds, black and white. I stop in the morning sometimes before work for a tall glass of carrot juice. Sometimes I go to lunch there by myself to take a break from work and just think. Me and my baby girl, Nyella, go sometimes for dinner. She sits, acting older than her seven years, and lets Richard serve her like a princess.

"How's Nyella, Florine?"

"She's doing wonderful, Richard, just wonderful."

"And work?" He winks and raises the eyebrow with the tiny scar. He knows that story, too. I have told him on many an occasion about how tired I am of working for the city.

"Oh, it's okay. I'm hanging in there."

Richard pauses and looks from me to Joan, waiting for me to make an introduction. He has no way of knowing this is different.

"Oh, Richard. This is . . ."

"Mrs Miller," she interrupts.

"Yes, this is Miss Miller," I say with a bit of sarcasm.

"*Mrs* as in married," she says.

"Any friend of Miss Florine's is a friend of mine. How are you, Joan?"

"Fine thank you," she says, barely raising her eyes to meet his.

"Well, you sure look fine, too," Richard says. "That hat brings out your skin tone. Damn, ain't nothing finer than a chocolate woman in colors." He brings his hands in close to Joan's face without touching her and she says thank you, returning back to her whispering self.

"Why do y'all come in here torturing me like this? Two fine sisters at one table on the same day. Uh, uh, uh. What's a brother to do?"

"Richard, you need to quit. What a brother could do is his job. Now, what's the special? No wonder it takes too long to get service, you stopping to harass all the women. I know you don't want me to go in the back and find Gloria."

I see a layer of worry peel off Joan's face and a bit of struggling smile begins at the corner of her lipsticked mouth when me and Richard laugh.

"Well, today is Caribbean day. We have jerked tofu, chicken if you like," he looks toward Joan, "with peas and rice, spicy greens seasoned with ginger and garlic, cornbread or wheat roll and ginger beer or island punch. The dessert special is date-nut squares."

Richard discusses the special with Joan, and I return to the forest of trees on the wall, trying to find a nice, quiet place where I can meditate on Joan's question. "The truth will set you free," I hear my mama saying to me. I was five years old and had just pushed my fingers through a small hole in the bedspread and tore it into the biggest hole I could make. This had been my mama's punishment for sending me to my room too early. "The truth will set you free," Mama says over top of Joan and Richard's voices. "Mama I don't know how it happened," I told her, "I just don't know." Minutes later, I confess, telling mama I knew how much she liked the bedspread but that she had got just what she deserved. When I think about it hard I can still feel the sting of mama's hand across my face. "And that's what you deserve," she said to me.

"Miss Florine," Richard's voice lulls, "what you having?"

"The special with tofu and cornbread and let me have some island punch."

Richard leaves and suddenly the world is awkward again. I try to return to the swirls of color amongst the trees on the wall when Joan pounds her silverware on the table.

"How long, Florine? Are we here to waste each other's time or to get this out? I *need* to know how long."

Need was the magic word. I had always acted on need. It had always been that way. Even as a little girl with fly-away bangs and pigtails sticking straight out, *need* had been my magic word. Playing in the backyard down home, making mud pies under my favorite oak tree. A pretty spring day, the dog, Buck, at my feet. I would get to playing hard, so hard that there was no other world to be seen and Mama would open up the screen door and holler for me to come on in the house. Who knows how many times she hollered. She could see me in full view at the edge of the yard, where yard turned into woods, but for some reason I never heard her until she said, "Florine, I need you to come in this house, right now." It was never the change in her tone or how loud she was or anything else but need. Grandmama told me she needed me to be the first one in the family to graduate from college and I left the creeks and the knobs of Blackfoot Branch, and made it so. And Simon, Nyella's daddy, hadn't been my boyfriend long, when one night in my apartment he pressed his hardness up against my thigh. He was tall, black as pitch dark, didn't talk much. He held me in his arms and put his face right up against mine, so close my eyes couldn't focus and said, "Reney, I know you want to wait since this is your first time, but I *need* to be inside you tonight." I allowed my breath to be taken by the fullness, the deepness of his kiss. The youth in my swaying hips sparked up like embers and burst into flame. That night I pulled back the quilts, laid across the bed and opened my legs like a sacrifice to fulfill Simon's need.

Joan's voice is a cracked, loud whisper and I turn my head just in time to see tears rolling off her cheeks. Tears well up in my eyes, too. It certainly would be easier if we were yelling and screaming, calling each other names. Be easier to just look at each other sideways from here on out, to whisper "I'm gonna kick her ass next time" to our girlfriends when we pass one another on the streets. But we decided to meet, to talk woman to woman, face to face.

I scramble through it all in my mind and stumble over some part of the truth, generic and sterile.

"Well, we met up a year ago. I mean you know we been knowing each other for a long time. We were just friends at first. Just friends. But we met up again."

"Where?"

"FoodCity's parking lot. He remembered me from when Nyella and Aisha went to camp together two years ago. We talked about the public school system and raising black kids up in it."

"So how did it happen, then?"

"Well, like I said, we just got to talking. It was cold out and we sat in the car and talked about the kids, his job, my job and what it's gonna take to uplift black people around here in general. He said he was getting a group of parents together to write letters and call on the school board to make sure they heard us loud and clear. So I finally told him that I really had to go cause Mama was waiting on me to pick up Nyella and if he got the group together to let me know. I told him where I worked and I was gone."

"And where do you work?"

The question makes me uneasy. No matter how new black womanish I am trying to be, I cannot have this woman coming on my job.

"I don't think that matters."

"Everything matters to me. Do you hear me? Ev-er-y-thing."

I just ignore the question and continue.

"So anyway, the next thing I know he calls me on my job and says he enjoyed talking to me that he don't get to meet many conscious sisters and . . ."

"Conscious sisters, what the fuck does that mean? The only *conscious* sisters he should have been worried about was his damn wife and daughter."

Here is Richard with the drinks just in time to bring some calm. I take a long drink of my island punch. I am surprised at the waft of rum I smell coming from Joan's drink. Evin don't drink.

Richard hears enough of the conversation and notices the red rims of both our eyes.

"Ladies, it will be just a few more minutes on your food. Here's an appetizer on the house."

Steam rises off the potato skins and makes a little spiral before it disappears somewhere up toward the ceiling. Richard stands behind Joan and mouths, "I'll talk to you later," to me.

"Thank you, Richard, you are so sweet."

"Sweet?" he says back over his shoulder. "I can't have you telling Gloria on me. It's a bribe." And he disappears into the kitchen.

"Conscious sister, my ass," Joan says and reaches for a potato skin.

"Well, all I know is what the man said. I'm just trying to be straight with you."

"Some tricks will fall for any *Dick* . . . Tom or Harry."

"Look, have you talked to Evin about this?"

"That's between me and my husband, but oh yeah I've talked to his trifling ass about it. Did y'all start fucking before or after he moved out of my house? I want to know cause I was fucking him too, and I don't want to catch no diseases. You say a year ago, huh?"

"The biggest part of our relationship began after he moved out."

"Relationship. Girl, fucking ain't no relationship. Thirteen years of marriage and a child is a relationship."

"It was much more than that."

"Couldn't have been. You were fucking my husband. Mine."

"Look, I'm trying to be as honest as I can and get this all out on the table once and for all."

"And I hope you are being honest. You better hope you are."

She takes a long sip of her drink and finishes off the potato skin. I ignore the threat and divide the potato skins on plates between us. We keep on eating while we talk. I find it funny that we are eating like old friends, while we untangle our intertwined worlds strand by strand.

Joan talks, her voice moves from stone cold to warm butter. I feel like she is the kinda woman that just can't have this conversation and is hell-bent on scratching out my eyes before we leave this table. Then, like she is one of my best sisterfriends and I want to put my arms around her so we can cry together. She talks and cusses herself to a clearing.

"I know you a woman and you hurting too," she says, tears streaming down her face again, "but this is my husband. Thirteen years. I love my man and I always will."

I want to tell her that I love him, too, but don't.

"I got a baby-girl to raise and I never even thought about raising her myself. Our kids are friends for God's sake! Aisha likes Nyella, a lot."

"I know, but none of this was deliberate on my part. It really wasn't. I always say I ain't looking for a man and I wasn't looking for him when he came along. I even told him not to call me no more but he kept on. I'm not that kind of woman. The kind that sets out to steal another woman's man. I'm not. And here he came, Mr Evin Miller, Mr Wonderful. Bright and intelligent. We read the same books. He was a forward-thinking brother. And he appreciated me. He didn't come off like some of the other brothers round here." I forget about Joan and am deep inside my own head, I think out loud. "It didn't happen slow, happened real fast, almost so fast I didn't know it. I didn't have time to think it all out. I didn't think. Said he loved to see a sister with a natural. Said he hated make-up and chemicals. The perfect man." I feel tears on my cheeks. Pent-up hurt runs down like a stream so salty I feel my skin drying taut.

"The perfect man? Your perfect man was my man. And he ain't never had no problem with my make-up or straight hair."

"I'm not talking about you and what you are or are not. I'm talking about me and what I was, what I am and what he made me think he was. He told me y'all was separating and that you were getting a divorce."

"Wasn't nothing ever said about a divorce. He said he was moving out cause he needed time to think some things over."

"Time to think, come on now do you really think . . ."

"I don't know what to think. What would you think after thirteen years? What would you think?"

"I don't know. I don't know what I would think and I don't know what I think right now.'

A sudden silence returns. We are both drained dry. I can feel an ache easing its way into my head and I try to will it away. I breathe in and out slowly, meditating with my eyes open to hold the headache at bay. "Always think good, soothing thoughts during times of stress," my doctor told me once. Then she topped it with, "and it wouldn't hurt to lose a few pounds." Fuck her. I don't need no bony-ass white woman telling me what to do on top of all this. I cram another potato skin in my mouth. My best friend, Gayle, told me once that I was a drama magnet.

She said that my life was ever evolving into fodder for any one of those day-time talk shows. Ricki Lake, Montel, Jerry Springer—she told me to take my pick. Maybe she was right.

Joan is in the middle of telling me about how she and Evin met and how in love they were when they married, when I jump up. Suddenly I need a break from this.

"Excuse me, I need to use the restroom."

I see Richard headed toward our table with the food but I have to get to the bathroom. I lock the door, pull my panties down and just sit on the toilet. I force a trickle out. "There, at least nobody could say I didn't tell the truth about that. I did use the bathroom." I sit there a long time with my panties still down around my knees. I remember another time when Mama caught me eating the candy that she was selling for church. I had wished myself invisible, wished the candy back in the box. I closed my eyes tight but opened them to find myself still there and still in trouble, the box still empty. This is like that. I lean back on the toilet like I'm sitting in a chair and just sit. No amount of wishing will make this situation go away and I can't take it back and mold it and change it. The done is done. I want to forget about Evin and stop waking up in the middle of the night crying. I want to finish this conversation, to clean my spirit like I think a real woman should and get on with my life.

This bathroom is decorated like a home bathroom instead of one at a café. I like the Egyptian-print wallpaper and the black Grade-A towels and washcloths. I flush the toilet and stand up. I breathe in deep the amber patchouli candle flickering on a tall pewter candleholder in front of me. I open up the medicine cabinet hoping to find something for my headache but it is empty. I take one last deep breath of patchouli, close my eyes over the candle, like it is lit just for me, and go back into the café. I've got to get on with it.

Richard is there with Joan and seems to have her almost to smiling again until she sees me turn the corner.

"Here she comes. Florine, we was beginning to wonder about you. Bon appetit, ladies. I'll come back and check on you."

Richard pats me on the shoulder and winks at me behind Joan's head. Without saying a word I dig into my jerked tofu. I sample a bit of everything on my plate and suck down some island punch. I'd better talk before my tongue stops working again.

"We both can't keep on doing this to each other. This has got to end. We are no longer each other's problem and I have got to get on with my life. If you and Evin get back together, fine with me. He is out of my life forever. I promise you that. I want you to know that. For once and for all, I am not your enemy. I don't want to fight you. I am tired, sick and tired. I just got too much on me. Can we please move on and clear this air? I mean as far as just between two sisters. I'm done with this, I really am."

"If you have told me one word of lie then you better watch your back. Cause I still love my husband and I'm going to be here when he comes back. But he's going to have to pay for what he did. And since you came to me as a woman then I want to believe you cause you was woman enough but I won't forget this. Can't."

"Nuff said then, good luck to you." She looks pitiful in my sight. All this man has done to her and her child, me and mine, and she still wants him back. All I can feel is sorry.

We finish out our meal in strange silence. She traces the rim of her glass with her finger between bites of spicy chicken and sips of rum drink. When she tips her plate to get the last bit of jerked chicken juice, I see she still wears her wedding band. I breathe deep through my nose, try to sort out the patchouli from the jerked seasoning, her musk from the greens. I look up for that little yellow bird on the wall. I imagine her a mama bird screaming out a woman's pain. I focus on the bright redness of her opened mouth.

No Ugly Ways

God don't like ugly but seems like sometimes he don't care for pretty none neither. My middle girl, she sure was a pretty child. Prettiest child in all of Kentucky. I cried when I saw her face. All that birthing pain lifted like fog. Hurt went clean on out of me. It was just something about how the light hit her face. I named her Pearl. I gave her that name cause it fit her. Course she had to go calling herself Ashay when she figured out she was African. Don't know why young folks got to do that. I've known I was a black woman and that my people came from Africa all my life but my name's always gonna be Willa Mae.

Pearl was the best looking one on the place, not that me and Ed didn't notice or love our other girls cause we surely did, but Pearl just shined like her name. Didn't matter what she wore—coffee sack or calico—she shined.

As she got older me and Ed never did treat her no different than the other four but she always acted a little bit different. Maybe cause she was the middle child, the special one. I bore two children before her and two after her. Odell and Marie before her and Spice and Belle after.

Pearl was always a timid child and real quiet. Her sisters came home with many a black eye cause they was taking up for her. She just wasn't born with no fight in her. I always told her about God and how he don't like no ugly ways but Pearl, I think she took me and God too serious.

Pearl and all the rest of my babies growed up to be good women, like I taught them to be. Odell married a schoolteacher and gave me and Ed three fine grandboys. They live up north. I keep their pictures right here on my coffee table. Marie lives in Hawaii with her husband, he's one of them islanders. I don't like that much but she's grown and he's a right nice feller and does her right. She expecting any day now. Spice is a college woman, getting her doctor's degree further down south at that Meharry College. And Belle is going to be married in the spring to an animal doctor and she's an animal doctor too.

Pearl, my poor baby, has had it rougher than most when it comes to menfolk. She had her first baby right at sixteen, little T. Earl.

We didn't know who T. Earl's daddy was then and Pearl never said til lately. We just figured it was some boy that forced hisself on her or maybe she gave in, not having the fight to say no. Boys was always coming around trying to get her to court 'em. She just never seemed interested. They all thought she was stuck up cause she was pretty but she never was. She just put all her attention toward God, always praying and carrying on. Just didn't seem to need no beau coming around for nothing. So when she came up pregnant, Dr Carson said not to keep on her about it too much cause she was on the edge of going on out her mind. The whole time she was in a family way, she just sat round staring out first one window then the other, looking up toward heaven like she was waiting for God to come on down.

She came to herself though after she brought T. Earl in the world. It was something we just chose not to talk about no more. So after she had T. Earl, she got her a secretary job over at the high school. She was doing good for herself til she met some good-for-nothing roustabout that was coming around the school selling cleaning supplies. My daddy always did tell me that some folks were born to pull the wool over other people's eyes and this feller, Sammy, was a natural born salesman. He could have sold my baby Pearl swampland in a desert. I don't know what made her fall for him.

I reckon she decided if God wasn't gonna come down for her that she had to go ahead and do something sides wait by the window and work and take care of that baby.

That Sammy brought her flowers, took her to fancy eating places, talked mess in both her ears left and right and treated T. Earl like he was his own. They up and married so fast it left us all spinning. Pearl's sisters didn't even have time to come in for the wedding. And I bout killed myself running around here like a chicken with its head a hanging, trying to make that girl a wedding dress, baking a cake and arranging for the ceremony with the reverend all in two weeks time.

It all turned out real pretty though. Pearl looked like a movie star in that dress that I made her. It was white, since it was her first wedding I thought it would be all right, and had ruffles cross the bottom almost touching the floor. I made her a crown out of Easter lilies and Ed bought T. Earl a little black suit. At three years old that little man gave his mama away. Even ole Sleazy Sammy looked all right that day.

Sammy packed up my baby Pearl and my grandbaby and moved them clean to Boyle County. Mind you, Boyle County is just two counties away but it's a mighty long ways between a mama and a child that's never been separated.

But things seemed to be going all right at first. Pearl stayed on at the high school here and brought T. Earl to me every day. Wasn't too much lost but then things started to change. No more than a year later, T. Earl stopped being so happy and Pearl commenced to avoiding me and her daddy. She'd let T. Earl out every morning and he'd have to walk the distance of the lane by hisself. She wouldn't come in and talk like she did at first. Some days I'd barely get to the door to see the boy coming through the gate and I'd see the dust flying behind her car in the other direction. We'd ask her if anything was wrong when we'd see her but she always said no. I had a bad feeling but put those feelings on out yonder on the fencepost cause I just knew that if Pearl needed us or was being mistreated she'd say so.

Everything always looked so nice and neat when we'd go over to her little place over at Boyle County. Made me so proud to see her in her own house, keeping things better than even I'd taught her to.

One day the phone rang and on the other end was Mrs Magdaline Howard. She lived in Stanford about halfway between me and my daughter. She said that she had heard through the grapevine at her church that Sammy was beating up on Pearl and she just thought I needed to know.

Now I don't know what made me do it but something like ice came straight over me and I jumped in Ed's truck and headed for Boyle County. I pulled up in Pearl and Sammy's driveway and T. Earl ran out to meet me.

"Grandma, grandma," he yelped and hollered dancing round and round in circles.

"Boy, settle yourself. You gonna make me dizzy."

I stepped up on the porch and had my fist balled to knock at the door when Sammy opened it.

"Well, hello Mama," he rolled off his tongue like he was singing a nasty song. "You sure looking good. What brings you over our way? Come on in."

My back commenced to crawling right up itself and I walked passed him into the living room. My Pearl had certainly made a right nice home for herself. It was clean, all decorated with praying hands and Jesuses. She had all type of Jesuses in her living room. Black ones, white ones, brown ones with some words in Spanish wrote cross the bottom. But that's my Pearl for you.

I didn't let on why I was really there and Slimeball Sammy rambled on and on.

"You took the warm right out the sun, Mama, I might have to marry you next. You sure you ain't Pearl's sister or something. It sure is nice to see you . . ."

"Mama, is that you I hear in there?" Pearl's voice came from the kitchen.

"Yes, baby, just thought I would stop by and see you."

"Mama, now coming way over here clean to Boyle County ain't just stopping by. Is everything all right? You all right? Is Daddy all right?"

Pearl comes through the kitchen doorway with worry cross her forehead, wiping her hands on her apron.

"No baby," I say moving my eyes up and down and from side to side across her looking for signs. "We all right. How y'all doing?"

"Mama, we just fine," my baby says, trying to convince herself as much as anybody. "I'm fine. T. Earl's feisty as ever and Sammy's fine, too."

T. Earl bursts in the room making a sound like a police.

"WHHHHHHRRRRR, WHHHHHRRR. Grandma, I'm the police. WHHHHHRRR, WHHHHRRR!"

"T. Earl, God don't like ugly," Pearl say to the boy. "Now do you see grown folks trying to talk?"

"Yes ma'am. Grandma can I sit beside you?"

"Sure you can, baby."

Sneaky Sammy leaves the room for a few minutes and

returns putting on his coat. I'm eyeing him all the time, too. I hope he can feel the heat from my stare.

"Mama, it's so nice to see you. You should visit us more often," he says to me. He kisses Pearl on the cheek. I see her resist a little then he pats T. Earl on the head, gives him a fake punch and goes on about his business.

"See you around eight, precious," he hollers back to Pearl through the door. "Keep supper warm for me. I got to make some home visits."

"Home visits?" I say. "At this time of night."

"Yeah, Mama, Sammy is an insurance salesman now. He don't sell cleaning supplies no more. He makes more money now and he can make a better living for us..."

Pearl goes on and on trying to explain her husband's profession but I don't pay her no never mind.

"Natural-born salesman if I ever did see one," I say under my breath.

"Pearl," I turn to her and say, "is Sammy," I use his right name this time, "treating you right? He ain't giving you or T. Earl no trouble is he?"

"Why no, Mama," she says, stuttering. "What makes you say that? Sammy is a perfect husband. Brings either me or T. Earl something new in here every night. He brought T. Earl a little police car just yesterday. He don't care none for my Jesus collection or me looking so much toward God for help but he's the one that bought me in the Puerto Rican Jesus just cause he knew I'd like it."

"Figures," I mumble under my breath. "And what about you T. Earl, how do you like Mr Sammy?"

"He's all right, Grandma. Did you bring me any cookies?"

He knows I did. I pull the peanut butter cookies from my pocketbook and T. Earl runs off to his room with them, foil and all.

"Boy you better put them cookies in there on that table til after you eat supper," Pearl says in her "I'll whip you" voice. She winks at me and we both giggle out of the sight of T. Earl. She's a good mama and I'm proud.

"Girl, well I guess I'd better head home before dark. I just came by to check up on you. You sure you all right?" She nods yes.

"Well, you know where your mama is if you ever need her."

I felt her tremble just the slightest bit when she hugged me but I took her word for what she was saying. All the way home, I felt an uneasy feeling about that situation but I never tried to place my finger on it too much any more.

We all went on like normal. I kept T. Earl almost every day while Pearl worked up at the high school. Just about every holiday as many of the girls as possible would come home. In between times they sent pictures and me and Ed spent a lot of time watching our family grow, even if it was more in pictures than it was in person. We didn't mind too much cause we loved one another and was glad that all our girls were happy.

Then one day, we get this phone call. Ed answers the phone. I've always been the one in the family to handle the problems. He never could handle much bad news. Never had much fight in him. Maybe that's where Pearl got it from. The news was on the other end of the line wasn't setting too well with Ed. He slumped in the chair and held out the phone toward me. Looked like he was having a heart attack. I could hear the boy screaming before I even put the phone up to my ear.

"Grandma. Grandma, please, please . . ."

I heard Sammy calling Pearl "a Jesus freak of a frigid bitch" then a loud cracking noise.

The phone went to a dial tone.

"What in the hell is going on over there?" Ed said looking somewhere past me, like he was talking to the wall.

"I don't know but we need to go over there and find out."

I guess some folks would have called the sheriff but getting the law involved ain't always a good decision when it comes to black folks' problems, even if it is an upright God-fearing family.

Ed and I pulled in the driveway just in time to see Sammy being carried out the house on a stretcher. Blood running all down all over everything white—the stretcher carrier's shoes, the sheets, even spots on the sidewalk. I could see he was dead. Then another body on a stretcher was brought out, blood dripping from her head. It was a pretty woman. They brought Pearl out next. She was wild-eyed like I had never seen her. They had handcuffs on her and she was still fighting, hollering and screaming. "Is the bastard dead? Is the motherfucker dead? Y'all better tell me if he's dead!"

T. Earl was at the edge of the porch huddled into himself with his eyes closed. He didn't even turn around to look at his mama. Ed, bless his heart, didn't know it was in him, finally got T. Earl to get hisself together and get in the truck.

We still go on. Always got to go on, you know. T. Earl's almost finished with high school. It's been nigh on ten years since that evening. Never thought a jailhouse would be a place where we'd gather the family. But I reckon family can be family most anywhere. When the girls come home we all go visit Pearl, especially on holidays. Pearl writes us from prison almost every day. Me, Ed and T. Earl go visit every third Sunday. Valley Prison's more than five hours away from here. We take a dinner basket in to Pearl, I mean Ashay, when they'll let us.

Once a month I make the trip down the road myself. Me and my Pearl, uh Ashay, have found that the gap tween mama and daughter is closing on up. I reckon I held her up so high, so long, that my eyes couldn't see. I guess I'm seeing her as a flesh and blood young-un now not some jewel out a necklace.

I've had a whole lot to think on over the last month. Last time I went down to see Ashay, I walked up to the table where she was sitting, in a little off-the-way room. The room was small as a matchbox. But they had it all decorated with flowery wallpaper and a little love seat and table and chairs like they was trying to fool somebody to believe it was a real living room.

She was looking as pretty as she ever was even in the prison's clothes. "Mama, please sit down," she says to me holding out her arms toward me like a preacher asking the congregation to rise. I sit down and she holds my hands, squeezes real tight, and begins to talk. "Mama, way back when I was sixteen, I was walking home from school," she says with her eyes rolled back, never looking me straight in the face. "Marie had stayed after school for band practice. And Spice was already home cause she was sick. A group of boys saw me . . ." She closes her eyes all the way when she got to that point. "They told me they was going to show me just how pretty I really was . . ." Tears was rolling down her face, running out tween those bright eyes what was closed. "Then they drug me over to old man Stuart's barn. I was saving everything I had, Mama, for a good God-fearing man, a preacher maybe but they took away everything I had saved . . ."

Seems like I knew what was next but at the same time I didn't know. Didn't want to know really. Tears got hold of me too. "Baby, it's all right, you don't have to tell me a thing. You done kept it to yourself all these years . . ."

Ashay cut me off. "Later that night, Mama, when y'all was sleep, I sneaked in the bathroom, filled up the sink with every cleaner I could find and rubbed myself raw, trying to get them boys' nastiness off me. But I felt it all the time, Mama. In my hair, on my breasts, deep inside me where I couldn't get the wash rag to. Down to my soul, Mama."

Then she told me who the boys were and told me

that little T. Earl was named after all his daddies. She would never know which one planted the seed for the child, so she named him "T." from the fact that two of them was Tommy Simms and Theodore Jones and the other three were Miss Earlene Givins's oldest boys, making the "Earl".

Told me she had waited all this time for God to strike them boys dead but he never came. Then she commenced to telling me all about Sammy. She commenced to rocking back and forth and I barely could understand her the tears was flowing so.

"Baby girl, it's gone be all right," I say trying to make a difference. "Open up your eyes and look at your mama, girl. It's gone be all right."

"No, Mama," she say with her eyes still closed. "I got to tell you it all fore it eats me any more. It's been inside me too long and I can't open my eyes cause I might stop in the middle if I do." She lays her head over on the table and unloosens one hand to put up under her head like a pillow. I stroke the side of her face like I did when she was little.

"When I met him, I thought the least my baby deserved was a substitute daddy but I married Satan himself. He bit a big chunk out of one of my breasts and my leg, anywhere where it wouldn't show. And late in the night when he came home from his meetings, he kicked me in the back with his boots while I'd be sleeping. And he forced hisself on me so many times . . ."

"Hush up, child," I say, "Shhh." But she just keeps on talking.

". . . he put what those boys did to me to shame, forced his privates in my mouth . . . He never did hurt T. Earl though, I guess I have the Lord to thank for that. So anyway . . ." she stops crying but brings her voice down to a hum ". . . I just kept the house clean, kept on decorating with as many Jesuses I could find. Then that day when he . . . when he died, Mama . . ." She raised her head up off the table then but still kept her eyes closed tight. "I walked in on Sammy huffing and puffing on top of that woman and her grinning up at him like she liked it. After everything he had to dish out. Right in my own living room, all my Jesuses looking down at them. Every ugly thing inside me moved right on up to the surface. I commenced to swinging all them Jesuses. The black one that was a wooden sculpture, the white ones in frames on the walls, the Puerto Rican one, too. I blamed all them Jesuses for letting him mistreat me. And now they were letting him get to his business with another woman right in front of them without even stopping him."

179

The way she described it was kinda like everything ugly got caught in her throat and extended out her limbs to her killing hands. She couldn't stop. It gave me cold chills but she said she even began to like the smell and sight of his blood after a few minutes. Said it felt like Sammy's blood was cleansing her. Freeing her up to step in where God nor those Jesus figurines wouldn't.

I held her a long time as she moved from crying to not crying. Weaving in and out of her feelings like a weaver hold of a loom. She even fell asleep a few minutes while I stroked the side of her head before they came in and told me it was time to go. She never opened her eyes to me, though. I kissed her forehead before I left and told her we was going to make it. She nodded her head.

Most days since, I ponder on what a different kinda mama could have offered the girl that I didn't. How a strong papa could have protected her. And sometimes when I'm by myself, I get to hollering up to God wondering, asking why he didn't rescue us all cause we was all waiting. Then I say to myself, "Willa Mae, you know God don't like ugly." Then I answer back sayin, "And pretty none neither, so what's left?"

About the author

Crystal Wilkinson
Photo by Jahi Chikwendiu

Crystal Wilkinson, who describes herself as a black, country girl, grew up in rural Kentucky, and teaches creative writing and serves as the assistant director of the Carnegie Center for Literacy and Learning in Lexington, Kentucky, as well as chair of the creative writing department for the Kentucky Governor's School for the Arts. She is a charter member of the Affrilachian Poets, a group of performing African-American poets from the South. Her work has appeared in various magazines and journals.

Blackberries, Blackberries is her first published collection.

The fonts used in this book are from the Garamond family.